CRAZYTIMES
SCOTT COLE

GRINDHOUSE PRESS

Crazytimes © 2020 by Scott Cole. All rights reserved.

Grindhouse Press
PO BOX 521
Dayton, Ohio 45401

Grindhouse Press logo and all related artwork copyright © 2020 by Brandon Duncan. All rights reserved.

Cover design by Scott Cole © 2020. All rights reserved.

Grindhouse Press #065
ISBN-13: 978-1-941918-68-5

This is a work of fiction. All characters and events portrayed in this book are fictitious and any resemblance to real people or events is purely coincidental.

No part of this book may be reproduced, stored in a retrieval system, or transmitted in any form or by any means, including mechanical, electric, photocopying, recording, or otherwise, without the prior written permission of the publisher or author.

Other titles by Scott Cole

SuperGhost
Slices: Tales of Bizarro and Absurdist Horror
Triple Axe

Dedicated to the people of Philadelphia.
More of this story is based in reality than you might think.

1

THE ALARM GOES off and I want to kill someone. This is true on most weekdays, and Mondays especially.

Not that there's anyone here to murder. Isa moved out months ago. No warning, no note, nothing. We ended up texting a little bit, once it became clear she didn't plan on returning. That's when she told me I would have seen this coming if I hadn't had my head so far up my own ass.

So now I'm all alone in this giant house.

It's way, way too big for one person—or at least too big for only me. There are three floors, plus a basement and an attic. It's an old Victorian twin, meaning it's narrow and attached to the house next to it, like a mirror image. Every house on the block is like this, although there are also rowhouses in the neighborhood, where each one is attached to the next all the way down the block.

There are rooms I rarely visit—rooms that probably never

would have been cleaned if not for her. Although, now, if I keep the doors closed and don't go into them much, they don't get too dusty.

I never would have even agreed to buy the house if not for Isa's nudging. Not that I'm blaming her or anything. We were happy here for a few years, and happy together for a few more before. We had plans at one point in time. Careers. Maybe a dog. This house.

I remember thinking we were going to turn the first floor into an art gallery. We had dreams of opening it up to the world—or at least our friends and neighbors—and exposing them to the greatest unknown or underseen artists we could find. Isa had a knack for that. Lots of connections and a mind-bogglingly good eye. It wasn't so much of a business venture as it was just something we wanted to do. But we also figured if anything sold, we'd put that extra cash toward the mortgage and hopefully pay it off that much quicker.

We thought about having concerts here too. Nothing huge, just some lo-fi house shows. If not in the first-floor gallery space, then in the basement, once we got that finished. In the summer, we'd throw parties in the backyard and gather around the fire pit when the sun went down. We planned to build taller fences and just have this little secluded space where we spent time with our friends.

"Our" friends. I haven't heard from any of them since Isa left. Guess they all made their choices.

I was planning, someday, to turn one of the third-floor

rooms into a massive library. Floor to ceiling bookshelves, except for two of the corners, which would house the most comfortable chairs we could find. We're both big readers.

I wanted a studio space too, where I could paint and maybe get back into sculpting, even if only on a small scale.

None of this ever happened, though. On the first floor there's a living room that nobody lives in, instead of an art gallery. The third-floor library is just a couple warped particleboard bookcases and a floor that can't be seen because of all the books piled haphazardly everywhere. The studio never happened either, despite the fact that it would've taken the least amount of effort to put together. I can't remember the last time I picked up a paintbrush. And the backyard . . . well, let's just say I'm looking forward to winter, so what little grass there is dies, instead of me having to go cut it.

I'll probably sell the place soon, and maybe someone else will start a gallery and build a fire pit and assemble a room full of bookcases.

It's way too much space for one person, and I just don't have the inclination to keep up with it. I don't really want the responsibility of homeownership, especially not without a partner.

I barely slept, but since there's no one here to murder over that, I might as well get up. I could fall back to sleep, but my boss probably wouldn't look too favorably upon that, the prick. So I roll off the sagging decade-old mattress, untangling my legs from the sheets, thinking, *Damn I really need to change these*, and catch myself in a sort of squatting position, just before face-planting on the floor. It's just the kind of jolt I need to fully—okay, partially—wake myself up and get the day started.

I shamble over to the bookcase where I rest my phone at night, a few steps away from the bed—an intentional choice to keep myself from staring into its glowing rectangle too deep, too late, in addition to being a measure designed to help me get the fuck out of bed in the morning. The alarm is still blaring, maybe even getting louder, although that could be all in my mind. Either way, I stumble in that direction, one eye half-open, the other still closed, and I mash the surface with my finger a few times until I hit the orange spot that makes the noise stop.

The bookcase is a short one, about waist high, painted black and covered with a film of gray dust, except for the spot I place my phone each night, which has slightly less dust. I can't even remember where we got it. Probably a yard sale or something, years ago. It's not in good shape—the back panel is barely hanging on and there are nicks and dents all over—but it serves its purpose.

The shelves are a mess of books I haven't gotten to yet, old receipts and other paper scraps, a few plastic toys, and a bunch of miscellaneous junk I've found in my pockets. There's a movie ticket, a crumpled paper sleeve from a plastic straw, and a pile of loose change. *Why haven't I done something with this crap*, I wonder, and promise myself I'll clean it all up later.

I check my notifications, hoping my boss has texted to inform me of some freak blizzard that rolled in overnight, cancelling work so I can go back to sleep, but no luck. Instead there's a weather advisory that consists of an icon I can't seem to figure out and a friend request from a bikini-clad woman who supposedly lives in some tropical place I've never even heard of. No snow.

I mean, I probably shouldn't have expected a freak snowstorm in September, but we can always dream.

I hear a loud boom outside and for a moment I think, *Shit, it's trash day and I forgot to take the can out to the curb.* But no, that's tomorrow.

I set the phone back down, keeping it plugged in even though it's fully charged, and head into the bathroom.

I nearly fall back asleep in the shower, just standing there comfortable in the warm water, not even washing myself. Then I snap out of it, not realizing how much time has actually passed, and give myself a quick once-over with the soap and scrub the smallest dot of shampoo into and out of my hair. When I climb out, that's when I really wake up, the cooler air shocking my system into full alertness. Fuck.

The wooden floor of the bedroom feels tacky to the soles of my freshly washed feet. I glance at the clock and see how late I really am. Double fuck. I do a quick sniff-test on some pants, throw on a definitely-clean-because-I-just-washed-it shirt, gather my things and run.

As I speed-walk down the street, adjusting the strap of my bag on my shoulder, I realize I forgot the leftovers I planned to eat for lunch. Oh well. It'll be dinner instead, and I'll have to buy

CRAZYTIMES

something this afternoon, even though I've been trying not to do that for a number of reasons.

I also realize the sky looks weird. There's a rusty haze hanging over the entire city. Maybe there *is* a storm coming. Wouldn't that be nice. A few hours late, but still. If it's something apocalyptic, maybe Rick will send us all home early. Hahaha. Right. He would never do that.

I dash past a Little Free Library, one of those dollhouse-looking things some people construct in front of their houses, offering books that people would rather pass along to strangers than keep for themselves. The idea of getting rid of books is unfamiliar to me, but I'm happy other people do it. I've filled plenty of gaps in my collection this way.

I stop and peruse the offerings at this particular one pretty much every day, looking for any new arrivals from my neighbors. Although I don't talk to most of them, I'm generally curious about what people are reading these days. In theory, these take-what-you-like offerings are supposed to be recommended books, although just as often, and maybe more so, it's a bunch of junk people are looking to get rid of. Still, I usually find something worth grabbing once a week or so, and it goes back to my shelves at home to sit among all the other books I haven't gotten around to yet. I definitely read, but I amass far more books than I have time to get through. There's a word for this in Japanese, but I can never remember it. In any event, I don't have time to stop and look now.

I'm a block away from the corner when I hear the bus coming. It's tough to tell which direction the sound is coming from, but the anticipatory movement of the people on the other side of the street are my tipoff. If the light changes, I might actually catch this one and not have to wait ten minutes for the next, which would be a small miracle and possibly get me to work close enough to on time that no one would care.

The light does change, but I don't catch the bus. It doesn't matter that I'm not quite to the intersection because the bus just zooms through the red light, its deep bassy horn blaring. The people on the other side of the street scream and wave their fists through the cloud of black exhaust the vehicle leaves in its wake. Guess we're *all* going to be late for work.

"What the fuck was that?!" an angry woman shouts when I get across the street. She's looking right at me as she says this, her eyes piercing, as if it's somehow my fault. It startles me for a second, but I realize she's just upset at the bus driver and needs to vent to whoever is within earshot. And maybe she's a little crazy. She is wearing a thick wool scarf, after all. In September. Maybe she was hoping for that blizzard too.

I move past her and a guy with a big beard screams "Motherfucker, motherfucker!" as I cross his path, and again I almost take it personally. Damn, I'm tired. As late as I'm going to be already, I'm gonna have to get some coffee in me before I get to the shop.

It's another twenty minutes before the next bus arrives. The car in front of it, an old powder-blue hatchback covered with political bumper stickers and dents, stops short at the light, and the scent of patchouli oil hits me in the face. The bus screeches to a halt, lurching forward before tapping the car's back bumper. The bus driver stands up and hangs half his body out the side window, screaming at the driver ahead of him, and I realize he probably would've gone right through the light if it hadn't been for the hatchback. The guy in the car has no reaction other than to bob his head along to the muffled music on his stereo, and the bus driver finally gives up and sits back down.

The angry woman on the sidewalk starts screaming again—*did she ever stop?*—because the bus driver hasn't yet opened the door.

"Let us on, you fuck!" she yells. "My taxes pay your salary!" I try to resist the urge to make a quizzical face at her remark, but I fail. When the driver doesn't comply with her demand, she decides to unravel the scarf from her neck—which to my surprise reveals a second scarf underneath—and wraps it around her hand. Then she punches the center hinge of the door a couple times, hard enough that it actually gives inward. The big beard guy steps up to help, sneaking his fingers in along the edge of the slightly-opened door, and slides it all the way open.

"I had it, you know," the woman snaps, upset at the man's oddly chivalrous act. He steps aside, making room for her to board first. She doesn't thank him. "I'm not fucking paying," she says to the bus driver, who responds with a hand gesture that seems obscene, although it's something I swear I've never seen before. "I already pay! Plenty!" she screams, halfway down the aisle.

The beard guy gets on next. He takes a dollar bill out—less than half the fare—spits on it, then slaps it against the plexiglass partition that keeps the bus driver safe from people like him. I imagine the guy's hoping it will stick, but it just falls to the floor instead.

"Good morning," I say. I always greet the drivers of whatever public transportation I'm taking—specifically because most people don't. I bend down to pick the beard guy's dollar up, but the driver yells for me to leave it, so I do. I wave my transit card in front of the sensor on the front of the fare box to pay, and he turns to look at me. His eyes narrow and the wrinkles alongside them deepen. Once again I'm taken aback by human interaction this morning. He looks hard into my eyes, almost through me.

"Boopy-doopy-doopy-doo," he says, soft and calm. Then he brakes, bursting into a cackle, and he slams a hand on the horn, even though the light is somehow still red. I move back to take a seat as he steps on the gas. The bus nudges the blue hatchback forward, then maneuvers around it, and into the intersection. Horns blare. A red pickup runs up a curb and crashes into a metal signpost. I grab a pole but still fall into the scarf lady, who's hanging out into the aisle even though the window seat next to her is unoccupied. She is not pleased. She starts screaming at me, but her words don't register as I try to right myself and scope out the seat farthest away from her.

It's gonna be one of those days, apparently.

2

BEFORE I KNOW it, we've left my mostly residential neighborhood and reached downtown, and I feel like I might actually get to work at a reasonable time. Late, sure, but not so late that it's offensive.

The pace of the bus slows on the Center City blocks, though, so we'll see. I look out the window instead of at my phone, always interested in people-watching and admiring the architecture of the city.

At a stoplight I see a guy holding a big sign on a stick. In large hand-painted block letters, it proclaims:

CLIMATE

CHANGE

IS REAL!

Then he spins the sign around to reveal the second half of his statement:

BECAUSE PENGUINS

*KEEP PISSING
ON ALL THE
GLACIERS!*

The guy has a huge grin on his face, and his big belly shakes as if he's laughing.

It's the sort of thing that makes me miss Isa. Hard. We used to talk, practically every day, about how crazy everyone else seemed to be. "You and me against the world," we used to say. Our home used to feel like an oasis in the middle of the city. As wild a day as either of us ever had, we always knew we'd be back there with the other one at the end of it, and we could relate our tales of strange encounters with the general populace to each other. Not that we thought we were better than anyone else—it just seemed like a lot of other people were falling out of touch with reality.

She used to wonder if there was something in the water. And if so, was it just a city thing? "No way," I would tell her. "Haven't you been to the 'burbs lately?"

I remember one day she told me about a guy who came into the bakery asking if they could cut a loaf of bread lengthwise, which she agreed to do, but after the fact, he tried to only buy the left half. When she tried to usher him out the door, he protested, claiming his wife would be by later to purchase the other side.

We made garlic bread that night. While the oven preheated, I told her about the guy who came into the print shop insisting we make duplicates of all his keys because he saw the word "copies" in the window.

The bus driver does his best to never come to a complete stop, but eventually there's so much traffic clogging one particular intersection that he's forced to halt his progress. Even then it takes a bunch of people yelling to get him to open the back door and let them out. It's technically two stops earlier than I need, but the way things are going, I decide to jump off at the last second too. The accordion door nearly closes on me, but I make it through.

It feels more humid downtown than it did in my neighborhood. Funny how that always seems to be the case. I guess it's all the concrete, all the buildings and machinery and steam grates venting underground utilities, the subway, and whatever else is down there keeping the city running.

A loud boom echoes in the distance, and for some reason the image in my head is of a crane dropping an I-beam. Construction is a constant down here, projects large and small. I doubt there's any land left, actually, but there's always a new building going up somewhere; it just happens where an old building used to stand. Maybe what I heard was actually a wrecking ball destroying some of Center City's architectural history. Sure, why repurpose an old building with some character when you can knock it down and start fresh with something flat and gray and boxy?

The coffee shop I used to frequent was turned to rubble a couple months ago for this reason. The owner of the building—I never figured out if it was just one guy or a boardroom full of people—decided he/they didn't like the art deco look of the building. So it's gone now, and a condo is supposedly going up in its place. Yay.

So I recently had to find a new coffee shop. No easy task these days, because fuck Starbucks. There are still a few others left, but frankly, some of them really *ought* to go out of business for what they try to pass off as coffee. I finally found one I like, though. It's actually more like an oversize kiosk in the lobby of one of the more historic buildings in town—an old department store, oddly enough—but hopefully that means it'll be here for a while. Who the hell knows. I run in and there's a line, of course. I wonder if all these people are late for their jobs too. If they are, they don't seem too worried about it.

There's a couple with two kids, a boy and a girl, in front of me. Tourists, obviously. Tourists who act as if they've never experienced the magic and the wonder of ordering food and drink at a coffee shop before. It takes them forever to decide what they want.

Thankfully, one of the guys behind the counter gives me a nod and a wink, acknowledging my presence and the fact that he knows my order, which he prepares while the tourists figure out what kind of milk the man wants his latte made with and the woman tries to determine the caloric differential between a cherry danish and a cinnamon raisin bagel. I pray she opts for the danish so the process doesn't get extended even further by having to make a cream cheese decision.

The barista's wink, on top of the nod? That's probably a little bonus. I've suspected this guy has a crush on me for a while

CRAZYTIMES

now—something I don't dispel because it often means he'll give me a size up or forget to charge me for a piece of coffee cake—although it could just as easily be to elicit a little extra tip money from my pocket. Either way, I recognize the fact that he's going to have my order ready to go by the time I get to the front of the line, which I appreciate even more than usual today.

There's an old clock on the lobby wall with ornately-shaped black metal hands, and by the time I get to the counter, those hands let me know in a very elegant, decorative, and borderline elitist way that I'm running even later than I thought. Fuck.

I've been saying "fuck" a lot this morning. I say it again as I grab my to-go cup and my finger slips past the edge of the brown paper sleeve and the cup wobbles in my hand and a little bit of hot liquid spills out of the lid and splashes over my thumb. Fuck, fuck, fuck.

My friend gives me a look, as if to say "be careful, honey," but doesn't apologize for overfilling the cup. I don't have time to make a big deal of things, though. I need to go.

"Hold up, muffin," he calls after me, and I spin back with what I'm sure is an unfriendly look on my face. I'm not in the mood for flirting, and I'm already trying to think up a good excuse to present to my boss. "You forgot your muffin," he says, smiling, handing over a white paper bag delicately folded along the top.

Okay, so maybe he's apologizing. I didn't order a muffin, but I'll happily take it. I'm starving. I smile back as I grab the gift. "Gotta run," I say. "See you tomorrow." And out the door I go, trying to make sure no more coffee burbles out of the lid as I walk as quickly as I can the rest of the way to work.

3

THERE'S ANOTHER CRASH in the distance as I approach the front of the shop. As usual, I don't go in that way. Instead I go down one alley, which connects to another alley, which leads to our back door. My desk is in the back anyway, plus this way I don't have to enter through the storefront and talk to any early-bird customers. I quietly crack the back door open for a peek inside before entering, hoping my boss is in his office and not standing by my desk wondering where I am. If I can get inside, sit down, and boot up my computer before we're face to face, maybe he'll just assume I've been there longer than I have. My coworkers won't say shit, after all the times they've each come in late and/or hungover, and I've covered for them.

Through the opening in the door, the coast looks clear. I slink in, and pad my way over to my desk, which faces a wall in the corner of the room. I raise my eyebrows and mouth the word "hi" to Jenny, wiggling a couple fingers from my coffee cup hand in her direction. She's got her headphones on and I cringe, thinking she's about to respond louder than I want, but she doesn't say a word, and I'm more thankful than she'll ever know.

I slip the strap of my bag off my shoulder and set it down on the floor, against the side of my desk, and slide into my chair as I fire up the computer. I sip some coffee as I tuck my feet under the desk and kick something soft.

It's my boss.

"What the fuck?" I say instinctively, and shoot myself backward on the wheeled chair. More coffee spills out of the lid and rolls down my fingers. "Fuck!" I hold the cup away from me so it doesn't drip onto my pants. Then I set it down on the corner of Jenny's desk and wipe my hand on my pants anyway because apparently I have short-term memory issues. Without saying a word, Jenny retrieves a paper napkin from her desk drawer and slides it over to me.

My boss is curled up, lying on his side beneath my desk. He dusts off the front of his white collared shirt, where it's stretched across his belly. That must be where my toes made contact.

"I hope that comes out in the wash," he says. "Where have you been, Trey? It's twenty after." He's not happy.

"I was . . . Wait, what are you doing?" I say. I'm pissed too. What the fuck is going on this morning?

"Well I'm certainly not getting any work done, that's for damn sure," he says. He seems perfectly comfortable where he is and makes no effort to crawl out from beneath my desk. Instead he repositions himself slightly, propping his head up with one hand. "After all, only so much can get done when our *highly revered* Production Manager hasn't yet shown up for the business day." He emphasizes the words "highly revered" in a way that's sarcastic and belittling.

"I'm sorry, Rick. The bus was late, and then it nearly got into an accident, and—"

"Nearly? *Nearly* got into an accident? So you're saying there ultimately was no accident, correct?"

"Like I said, I'm sorry. But I'm here now. If you wouldn't mind coming out from under there, I can get to work immediately."

"Oh, I don't think so," he says. What the fuck is he talking about?

"Umm. Okay." I turn toward Jenny, but she's doing everything she can to ignore the entire scene around her and stay focused on the music in her ears and whatever's on her screen. I'm a little pissed she didn't warn me about Rick hiding under my desk. She's got my number. She could've texted me a heads-up.

"No, I think I'm just going to stay under here today and make sure you do your job. Apparently someone has to keep an eye on you."

I'm speechless. I'm starting to wonder if I really did wake up this morning. Maybe I'm still in bed, dreaming. I squeeze my eyes shut tight and tell myself to wake up. But when I open them, I'm still sitting on the rolling chair under the fluorescent lights with a hand that smells like fresh coffee.

4

OVER THE NEXT couple hours, I bury myself in my work, and several times I even forget that my boss is curled up by my feet.

From time to time, I take my eyes off the screen and focus on something three-dimensional. I keep my desk in much better shape than my home. It's very neat. No miscellaneous trash, no scraps of paper. Just the essentials for work and a couple little toys to keep me sane. I've never decorated my desk beyond a few knickknacks, never put up any photos or anything. I'm very friendly with my coworkers, but I'm happy to have my boss know as little as possible about my personal life, and my personality outside of work. We're just different types of people, and we don't mesh well.

We don't even mesh well when it comes to business, but I suppose that's true of a lot of people and their shitty bosses.

I take a minute to stare at one of the pieces of plastic on my desk, a three-and-three-quarter-inch action figure depicting Henry Bemis from that *Twilight Zone* episode where the world ends and he finally has time to read all the books but then his glasses break. It's painted black, white, and gray, like the show, and it kind of blends in against the gray wall behind it.

What a drab environment, I think. Gray walls, gray metal desks, black faux-leather chairs. Lots of paper, all either brilliant white or bright white or off-white or "natural," which is print-shop-speak for cream. I went to school for art and design. I always wanted to work somewhere bright and colorful and fun, but I ended up here. Such is life, I guess.

Maybe I should look for another job. I could use a change. I've been here for over a decade now and if it's not the same old bullshit every day, it's just new and different bullshit, like a boss hanging out under your desk.

I've spent the bulk of the last two hours troubleshooting the files for a booklet that a local furniture company has asked us to print. It's potentially a big account, and this is our first job for them, so we've got to do it right. Unfortunately it looks like the guy they got to design the thing has little-to-no experience working for print. It's the sort of thing I'm seeing more and more of these days. There are all sorts of transparency and layer issues in the file, not to mention this guy didn't pull out his bleeds, account for any creep, or any of the things a booklet designer should automatically know to do. His fonts aren't even embedded. My guess is this guy went to school for web design and never took a print production class, or more likely just taught himself Photoshop at home and decided to call himself a designer. Whatever. This is my life, and it makes the hours pass, I suppose.

The furniture company is called Sybbling Brothers, which makes me chuckle. But the smile fades from my face as I'm reminded of my own siblings. My brothers. I was born one-third of a set of triplets. My brothers died when we were young, but I survived.

I deal with guilt—survivor's guilt, they call it—something that rears its ugly head from time to time, and without warning. I was seeing a therapist for a while—something Isa had encouraged—but I haven't made an appointment since she left. I manage, for the most part, but every now and then it hits me like a wave of depression, even though logically I realize there's nothing I could have done all those years ago as a child.

"Hey," Jenny says, thankfully jolting me out of the thought that could easily get me spiraling. I turn around and she's standing up at her desk, wearing a wrinkled orange, black, and gray plaid shirt, unbuttoned, with a band tee underneath. Something demonic, but I don't recognize the logo and there's no chance I'll be able to figure it out without her thinking I'm staring at her breasts, so I don't bother. She's also got a black knit winter hat on, which is typical for her, though I don't understand why some people wear winter hats year-round. She's wearing her glasses with the white frames too, with the arms tucked under her ears, which are tucked under her hat. The white frames remind me that it's only Monday. She has five pairs of glasses that she wears to work—white on Mondays, three gradually darkening shades of gray for Tuesdays through Thursdays, and then, surprisingly, red on Fridays. I wonder what she wears on weekends.

"Contacts," she says.

"Huh?" Wait, what? Did I say something out loud?

"Con-Tex," she repeats. "That big brochure job? They just approved their proof." She hands me the job jacket, a plastic sleeve with paperwork and our copy of the proof inside, so I can put it into Production. "Anyway, I'm going to lunch." She organizes a few things on her desk, grabs her purse, and steps toward the back door. "You need anything?"

"No, I'm good," I tell her. "Probably just gonna work through lunch today. Gotta make up some time, ya know." I roll my eyes at her, hoping my boss can't see the look. Jenny smiles, then she's out the door.

Rick, under my desk, clears his throat.

I decide to get up and go toward the front of the shop to make sure things are under control. Jenny and I work in the back, handling all the technical stuff—job intake, file prep, and scheduling, mostly—back there, while the others—Kia, Andre, and Joseph—do the actual printing and finishing work, cutting down sheets of flyers and postcards, folding brochures, saddle-stitching booklets, and all that. I used to do that work myself, years ago, but thankfully I worked my way up to a sort of management position. I'm grateful for that at least. If I was still standing over a booklet-making machine feeding short stacks of paper into it, one book at a time for half the day, and cutting down stacks of 250 or 500 business cards every ten minutes for the other half of the day at this point in my life, I'd probably kill myself.

Thankfully Kia and Andre are young and eager to get some experience under their belts, and don't mind doing those sorts of things. I bet they will in a couple years, though, and at that point it'll be up to me to find their replacements. Unless, like I said, I find some other job. But that will probably have to wait until after I sell the house.

Joseph handles the front counter, and all the customer service stuff I'm happy to take absolutely no part in. We're located right on the ground level of a slightly less traveled street, so it's convenient for a lot of people to just stop in and pick up their jobs. Joseph takes their payment, hands them their boxes, and sends them on their way.

In the middle of our space is a large Production floor. We've got three digital printing presses and a variety of very industrial-looking finishing machines—a pair of bulk cutters, or guillotines, a couple pedal-activated saddle-stitchers, a scoring and folding machine, another that folds without scoring, an offline booklet-maker, a perfect-binding setup, and more. It's a decent little setup. We're a small business, but lately we've been growing—although I haven't seen any growth in my paycheck. That's something I'll be talking to Rick about at some point, although today is clearly not the day for it.

Kia is changing the blade on the guillotine when I get up front. It's a mammoth machine that serves a single purpose—

CRAZYTIMES

cutting stacks of paper. There's a dial on the front that adjusts the gate at the back—a guide that keeps the paper stack in position—and there are two square buttons on the front panel. One on the left, one on the right. They both have to be pressed at the same time in order for the machine to cut. That way you don't accidentally bring the blade down while you've got one hand inside adjusting where you've got your paper stack positioned. So, bring down the clamp with the foot pedal, then push both buttons within a second of each other, and *voila*. Blade comes down, blade goes back up. Paper is cut. Reposition your stack, step on the pedal, push the buttons. Repeat. Repeat. Repeat. Repeat. Forever. Forever.

It's a good thing that safety feature is built into the machine. The act of cutting is kind of mind-numbing after a few dozen chops, and it's easy to get lost in one's thoughts.

"Blade was dull," Kia says.

"I can see that," I tell her. The blade itself is about three feet wide and maybe six inches tall, with one edge that's insanely sharp, even when we consider it too dull to do what we need it to do. The process of swapping it out for a sharper one involves a contraption with two cylindrical handles that latch onto the blade perpendicularly. Safety first. "How's the Flenderson's job coming along?"

"Good, actually," Kia says. "We're halfway done already. Andre is boxing them up now while the rest of the covers are printing, then I'll score them and he'll jump back on the booklet-maker."

"Cool." I glance over at Andre and we nod at each other, then I call up to the front of the shop. "Everything good up there, Joseph?" He nods too, and takes a sip from his coffee mug while holding an upturned thumb high in the air. "Okay, everyone. You know where I'll be. Go team."

I get back to my workspace, which is separated from Production by a wall and an open doorway, and immediately hear a *scritch-scritch-scritch*. My boss looks like a dog in a bed beneath my desk. I don't even know what to say to him anymore. I was already questioning his sanity, but now it looks like the results are in.

"Everything okay down there, Rick?" He doesn't respond, unless you count the pawing at his neck to relieve his itch. "You need some water or something?"

Maybe he's off his meds. I don't know what his ailments are—we're not exactly close—but I've seen him pop pills at his desk on many occasions. Although I suppose they could just as easily be something he doesn't have a prescription for. Or they could be Pez for all I know. I really don't care, actually, as long as my paychecks continue to clear.

There's a tiny kitchenette at the opposite end of the room—really just a sink and a couple shelves. I find a shallow plastic bowl and fill it from the faucet, then bring it back and set it down beside him underneath my desk. He immediately swipes at it, spilling water all over the commercial-carpeted floor. I leave it and sit back down. I have shit to do.

A few minutes later I'm ticking away at my keyboard, responding to various emails, and I feel him poking at my feet. Exhausted by the entire situation, I tap my toes in an effort to get him to stop. He groans. Or is he purring? Then the scratching starts back up, and he must be leaning against part of my desk because I feel it shaking ever so slightly. Henry Bemis falls over, and I grab the figure to stand him back up, then realize he's probably just going to topple over again.

Rick touches my foot again and suddenly the urge to kick my boss has never been greater. Yeah, it's been there for years, but bosses tend to think unfavorably toward acts of physical violence, particularly when they're aimed in their direction. So I decide to slouch down in my chair and glance down past the near edge of my desk, past my lap, and I find him sucking on the edge of my shoe, moaning like a dog with a bone.

I kick. And it feels good. The motion detaches him from my foot and I roll back.

"Seriously, Rick. What the fuck?!"

His eyes are wide with surprise. Then, in a burst of energy, he scrambles out from under the desk and darts across the floor like a beast.

"Gimme your foot! Gimme your foot!" He's screaming at the top of his lungs and bouncing around in circles on two feet and one hand. I've never seen him move so quickly. He's scratching away at his neck with the other hand. His shirt is untucked now, and his collar is disheveled. His neck is raw where he's been scratching, red and purple, covered with crisscrossed lines. "Gimme! I need your foot! Your foot! Your foot works for *me*, goddamn it!"

He launches at me again, but I manage to dodge him, falling out of the chair in the process. I scramble to my feet as Rick holds his position. I think he *is* purring.

I hear a big boom in the distance, somewhere outside. It's close, though. It feels like it shakes the building. For a second it reminds me of the earthquake we had a few years ago. Then I hear Joseph yell something from the front of the shop, and my concern instantly triples. Was there a car accident right outside? Did a car actually crash into the shop?

Rick lunges at me, but I see him coming and swoop around behind my chair and use it as a barricade. Then I ram it into him, knocking him back on his ass. The back of his head clunks against the front of my desk, a perfectly placed shot that knocks him out instantly. This isn't the movies, though—he's only out for a second, then he's trying to get back to his feet.

"What the hell are you doing, man?" I yell. I wonder if there's any sense in trying to reason with him, or if I need to call the police or a doctor or someone. I think he's married, but I've never met his spouse and wouldn't know how to get in touch with anyone who wasn't a client.

He growls and comes at me again, and I slam the chair into him a second time, now a little harder, and it sends him back into the desk again. My monitor tips forward at the same time and falls face-first onto the top of the desk, just as the back of Rick's neck collides with the edge. He's out, and I'm hoping he stays unconscious for at least a few minutes so I can figure out what to do about him. After I assess what's going on up front, that is.

I realize I'm still holding the action figure, so I tuck it into my front pocket and dash up to the front of the shop, where I find Joseph standing at the window. The huge pane of glass is covered with a film of creamed coffee, and he's standing there drawing stick figures in the opaque coating. They look like they're fucking. He's biting his lower lip and giggling to himself like a mischievous little kid. He's scratching his neck with his other hand.

Andre and Kia have disappeared. Maybe Joseph scared them off? I'm about done with this day myself, and I haven't even had lunch yet.

"Joseph? What's going on, buddy?" I ask as I approach, careful not to startle him.

Again I wonder/think/hope I'm still asleep, stuck in some bizarre dream I can't seem to wake up from. But I know that's not the case. This is actually happening. It's real, and it's real fucking weird.

Maybe Isa really was onto something when she said she thought there was something in the water. For a while now, the world has felt like it's becoming a more bizarre place every single day.

"Crazytimes," she would declare. "We are living through the Crazytimes."

Joseph is scratching at his neck like Rick was. The skin is raw, and there's a web of purple markings, almost like netting. The spaces between the lines look like yellow blisters, and as I get closer, I realize they're moving. Pulsating. Did Rick's neck look like this? I saw some lines but assumed they were scratch marks. This looks like something more than that.

Suddenly, the skin of Joseph's neck and shoulder area bursts outward, as if several popcorn kernels had just popped beneath the surface of his flesh, exploding to the size of tennis balls. The sight staggers me backward and I nearly lose my footing.

Joseph yelps, something that sounds more like delight than pain, then he smashes his head hard into the oversized window, shattering it instantly. He laughs as the shards of glass rain down on his head and shoulders, carving dozens of fresh red lines into his skin. Then he turns around to face me, laughing like a maniac.

His eyes are wider than I've ever seen them before. He starts spinning them in circles as his laughter gets even louder. Soon he's screaming his laughter in something akin to an over-the-top comedic performance—something that starts out funny then gets annoying before becoming absurdly funny once again. This remains serious, though.

Kia jumps out from somewhere—I don't even know where she could've been hiding—and she's got the guillotine blade with her. The rig to handle it is still attached, but the guard that covers the sharp edge is gone. She's holding the blade by one of the cylindrical handles, off to her side, spinning the giant knife vertically like a police officer's baton. I'm impressed she has the strength to do this. Those blades are heavy, and I doubt I could swing one the way she is.

Without a word, she runs to the front of the shop, stepping on a paper carton when she gets there—it still has the yellow plastic strap around it, so it's full—which helps her propel herself over the counter, and in one smooth motion, she swings the blade at an angle and takes the top half of Joseph's head clean off, from his jawline on one side to just above the ear on the other. His laughter wails to a stop while Kia's follow-through spins her around and embeds the blade back down into the countertop. Joseph's arms shoot out and wrap themselves around Kia's torso, but she breaks free of them easily as blood spurts violently from what remains of Joseph's head, and his body collapses. She turns back and stomps on his chest and stomach several times, although the effort is wasted. His body convulses as blood puddles beneath and around him, and he's dead in a matter of seconds.

I breathe a sigh—something that's more loaded with fear and confusion than relief. A gust of air blows in through the window, rifling the pages of the paper company-supplied calendar on the wall and knocking a couple bits of glass free from the window frame. Kia just stands there, looking down at her coworker's corpse, breathing heavily.

"What the fuck?!" It's Andre, who also appears from out of nowhere. Seems to be the phrase of the day. I turn around and see the shock on his face, which I'm sure matches the look on mine. I want to say something in response, but before I can, I realize Kia has dislodged the guillotine blade from the counter, and is darting toward Andre.

All I have time to scream is "No!" before she swings it at

him horizontally like a baseball bat, severing his left arm at the elbow, and getting stuck in his ribs. She issues a primal scream as Andre's shock doubles, his eyes wide at the sight of his arm on the ground and the blood spurting out of his wounds. He drops instantly.

"You're next, fucko," she says, turning toward me and giggling before placing a foot on Andre's chest and ripping the blade violently out of his side. The wet cracking sound is sickening, and blood splats against the dingy gray wall.

There's another scream in the back. Rick is awake again, and he quickly makes his presence known in the doorway. His neck and shoulders have now swollen and bubbled outward the same way Joseph's did, but Rick's mutation appears even larger. He looks monstrous, his frame now expanded so large and irregular on one side that his shirt has been torn to shreds.

There's a loud boom outside, and Rick responds to it immediately, babbling something—it's not even words—as saliva and what looks like some sort of purple slime spill out of his mouth. Kia reconfigures and goes after him instead of me. Terrible as it is, I'm thankful for the extra time, though I don't know what my next move is.

Kia screams and brings the guillotine blade down in an arc, right into the center of Rick's head. As much as I've always disliked my boss, this is a shocking thing to behold, as his head splits perfectly down the middle, each half wilting to either side. Several of the bubbles on his shoulders explode, spraying purple and yellow liquid all over the walls and floor. And all over Kia too.

She explodes into laughter herself. It's maniacal. Then she turns her head back and makes eye contact with me once again. Her eyes spin. My only choice is to run out the front. But before I do, she pulls the blade up out of Rick's neck and positions it horizontally with both hands, just in front of her shoulders. Then, wide-eyed, she raises her chin, exposing her neck, and drags the blade across it, back and forth, back and forth. It's only then I see the purple markings and the raw skin on her too. Blood, along with purple and yellow slime, all spurt from the wound she creates, spattering her arms and pouring down the front of her shirt, creating new puddles at her feet. One of her shoulders bursts outward during the process too.

She only moves the blade a few times before life evaporates from her body and she drops to the floor.

And suddenly it's quiet in the shop except for the sound from outside and all I can do is try to catch my breath. Easier said than done.

5

TEN MINUTES LATER I'm still standing there. I haven't moved. My feet feel like they're glued to the floor. Everyone around me is dead, and I don't know what to do.

I pull my phone from my pocket, but I have no signal. It's never been strong inside the shop, but it's never been nonexistent either. Finally I feel able to lift my feet, and I'm thankful we still have a landline at the shop, and I go up to the front counter and grab the phone on the wall, but it's dead. No dial tone, nothing.

I have to get out of here. I have to call the police. I'm shaking. There's blood everywhere. Will the cops even believe this? What do I do? What the fuck is happening?

From the corner of my eye, I see two small clouds of smoke roll past the now-vacant window frame up front, floating down the street like traffic, but in the opposite direction. Maybe someone's smoking next door? But if so, how could they not have heard what just happened here? How could they not have come to investigate or call for help?

When I go look, all I see is a very large naked woman running down the street, as if she's chasing the puffs of smoke. There's currently no traffic, so she's free to run right down the middle of the road. She's going full speed, with her breasts in her hands, pointing them threateningly like a pair of loaded guns at anyone who looks in her direction.

Her neck looks raw and covered with the same purple web pattern I've seen a few times now—enough to know I better steer clear. Thankfully she passes by without noticing me, and she continues down the street, barefoot, naked, and crazy. And of course she's laughing like a lunatic.

I hear another boom in the distance, followed by sirens. So whatever's going on, maybe the police already know. I hope.

How widespread is this insanity? I wonder. I mean, there's obviously something going on, some kind of sickness, some kind of plague. I've reached that conclusion already, no need for anyone else to confirm it. At the very least, the diseased purple look on people's necks seems to be a tipoff on who to avoid. I hope I can count on that.

I step through the front door slowly and look both ways down the street. It looks safe enough now that the crazy naked lady has passed, so I go. Across the street is an alley, and I think that'll be a quick route to the next block over, but when I get there, there's a bunch of guys standing halfway down it. There's six of them. Three look dirty and haggard, probably homeless, wearing far too much clothing, all of it soiled. The other three are young businessmen in what appear to be expensive pin-striped suits.

I stop dead in my tracks, and jump behind the corner, and thankfully they don't notice me. I wait for a minute and watch, peeking around the building. They're all laughing uncontrollably. Each of them has their back against one or the other brick walls of the alley, all of them half-squatting. And I watch as they all produce mason jars from somewhere, then pull their pants down, and in near-unison, shit into their jars. I catch a whiff of it from where I'm standing and gag. Still laughing, they replace the lids, sealing their waste inside. Then, after one of them counts one-two-three, they all run out the far end of the alley, into the street, and throw the jars at storefronts and bystanders.

I decide to head in the opposite direction.

6

A BUNCH OF the buildings in this part of town are abandoned, or at least closed up and not being used. Someone owns them, I assume. The common consensus has been that two or three different people own most of the real estate in the city, and in some cases they hold onto buildings until the going rate has risen high enough that they're either worth selling or worth renting out at exorbitant prices.

I slink down the block, doing my best not to be noticed. There are people scattered about, but no cars, and when I get to the end of the street I can see why. Someone has made a makeshift pile of office chairs near the intersection. There are a few different styles, and many of them are broken to bits.

"Oh yeah?" a voice calls out from far away. "Well how about this?"

I look up just in time to see a middle-aged woman in a blue and white dress pushing an office chair out a window, from eight or nine floors up the high-rise on the corner. It sails down, spinning the whole way, and crashes onto the pile at the end of the street.

Something else crashes in the distance at the exact same moment, making it seem as if the chair's impact echoes across the city. Something smells like it's on fire.

She howls with laughter and smacks her palms together a few times like a baby who's just learned how to clap.

"Boooooo!" screams a younger guy wearing a pink tie around his head like a bandana, and nothing else, mockingly, from a window across the street, about the same number of floors up. "Check *this* out!" Then he pushes one of his own chairs out from high above and it crashes into the pile too.

The woman flips him off and says she's going to kill him. I decide to make a swift exit from the scene and slip down an alley.

On the next block, I encounter a disheveled-looking man in a trench coat sitting on the sidewalk, smearing something light brown on his hand with a knife. I'm initially revolted by what I think I'm seeing, but then I notice the peanut butter jar on the pavement beside him. He goes into a glass jar of strawberry jelly next—I recognize the brand as the same kind I buy—and adds a layer to his hand, attempting to spread it as evenly as possible.

There's a patch of gravel in front of the storefront next to the one he's leaning against. It appears to be there temporarily, until the sidewalk paver can be replaced. An older woman, lean and muscular, is squatting beside it, picking through, stone by stone, bringing each one to her mouth. She gives each rock a tiny, delicate kiss, before inserting it into her mouth, at which point she appears to bite it with her molars, testing it like some old-timey prospector, before either swallowing it or casting it into the street. She scratches at her neck and chuckles softly to herself between each inspection.

I avoid all of these people by slipping down another alley. The next block over is surprisingly quiet.

A few minutes later I find myself in front of Wok Around the Clock, a twenty-four-hour Chinese restaurant I've been to a million times, although not recently, since I've been trying to save money and also watch my sodium intake in an effort to lower my blood pressure. I imagine getting a new job would likely reap the same benefits. I'm sure my BP is fine right now, though, since there's nothing stressful going on in my life. And I sure could go for some spring rolls.

I drop down low and creep toward the door. It's glass. Peeking through, it looks like all is calm inside. There are a handful of patrons eating lunch, and a couple servers delivering large platters of food to a few others. Seems like it could be a safe haven. But how? Seems like the whole city has gone crazy. I stand back up and slip inside quietly, just in case.

"Table for one?" a very tall middle-aged woman with short hair says immediately, and louder than I would have expected. It startles me. She's the owner. I recognize her, but she probably doesn't remember my face from the last time I was here, over a year ago. People don't ever seem to remember me when I'm not with Isa.

I nod, keeping silent while I continue to assess the surroundings. She motions for me to follow her, then leads me to a booth. I slide in, and she hands me the menu, opened to a page labeled "Chef's Specialties." I thank her, then pretend to look at the menu, but instead look over the top of it, examining the other diners to see who has purple streaks or swollen blisters or rashy, itchy necks. I see no such evidence, and realize how hungry I really am. One of the other patrons receives their meal and it smells amazing.

Suddenly someone leans around from behind me. "Tea?" she asks, more like a command than a question. I'm startled again, but she's my server, a young but stern-looking woman with long, straight black hair, and she's got a steel teapot in one hand. With the other, before I even respond, she reaches across my table setting and turns a white ceramic cup over, then fills it with hot liquid. The cup has no handle, but features ridges to nest one's fingers comfortably into.

"What would you like?" she says, monotone and emotionless. I hesitate, barely. "You need a minute?"

"Uhhh, no," I say. "Just an order of spring rolls."

She looks at me, as if to say "Really? That's it?" but doesn't utter another word. Instead she writes the order on her pad, then grabs the menu from me and pushes through the swinging door that leads to the kitchen.

I'm confused. I continue looking around the dining room, examining the faces and necks of the other patrons. Some start to notice, and clearly take offense at my invasion of their privacy,

CRAZYTIMES

but nobody says anything about it. I get a few looks, but that's it. Nobody stands up and tries to fight. Nobody screams or laughs or yells the word "fuck" or starts slamming the walls or anything. Everybody is calm. I try to act as if I'm just admiring the decor—the giant painted depiction of an ancient Great Wall, the large embossed Mandarin characters painted gold against the shimmering red wallpaper, the potted chrysanthemum tree in the corner, the paper lanterns dangling from the ceiling.

So maybe everything is fine? I did just see what I thought I did, right? A bunch of people just got killed where I work, right? And all the crazy people outside? So why is everybody going about their business here? Why is no one freaking out? Have they all been holed up here all day? The door wasn't locked, and most of these people look like they've just stopped in for a meal, like they would on any other day.

Another server, a tall man, passes by my table, and I stop him, asking if they have a phone I can use.

"Not working," he says. "Service is out all over town."

How would he know that unless he's been outside? Out among the crazies. The murderers. The guys shitting in jars and throwing them at people and the naked ladies with mutating bubbly necks.

My server returns with my spring rolls and sets the plate down without a word, then moves along to fill teacups at another table. The other server, whom I asked about the phone, goes through the door to the kitchen, and I could swear I see him grab his neck before the door swings back.

I panic. Maybe it's okay, though. Maybe he's just stiff and giving an achy muscle a comforting squeeze. Too tough to tell for sure, but everything seems low-key here. I take a deep breath, inhaling the aromas of the room, and bite into a spring roll. The wrapper crackles and flakes all over the plate and the red paper placemat beneath it.

Someone in the kitchen screams something. I can't understand what, and I tense up, but then I hear others laugh in response. Things quiet down almost immediately, and the two servers reappear with smiles on their faces, so I assume all is well. Someone just told a joke.

I take another bite and glance around the room, and that's when I realize things aren't quite right after all. At one table, a couple has produced a bottle of ketchup and a jar of mayonnaise, and the woman is squeezing ketchup in a spiral pattern on top of her noodles, while the man is reaching into the mayo jar with as many fingers as he can fit, before throwing dollops of it onto his chunks of orange something.

In the opposite corner, a man is slicing across the palm of his hand with a knife and letting it drip into his soup with a smile. A little boy is on the floor, licking the carpet. And a woman has been calmly tugging at her own hair, plucking it out in small batches. She's half bald at this point. I hadn't noticed any of this before, somehow.

As I witness all of this, I reach for my teacup and take a sip to wash down my spring roll. Then I spit the liquid out, spraying the seat across from me.

"More pee?" the server with the teapot says, appearing again as if from nowhere. She's scratching her neck and now I can see the purple marks creeping out from beneath her collar. They were hidden by her hair before.

I swing my body sideways, sliding my legs out so I can deliver a push-kick to her midsection with both of them, sending her stumbling toward the center of the room.

There's another scream from the kitchen, and a clattering sound as dishes fall and a cook comes barreling out, both hands firmly grasped around the wooden handle of a wok, brandishing it like a weapon. He looks crazed, his eyes spinning violently in circles, and his shoulders are hunched and severely bubbled as if he had stashed a half dozen baseballs under his shirt. Purple streaks crisscross his neck, encasing yellow blisters in a grid. He begins swinging the wok, swiping at every person in his path.

The boy on the floor stands up, giggling as he points at the cook, just before the wok clangs across his head. The cook takes aim at the teapot lady next, but she raises the steel pot up in defense. The metal on metal collision is loud, and when the lid is dislodged, hot piss splatters across the center of the room. The server laughs like it's the funniest thing she's ever seen.

In unison, the other patrons stand up, and the place explodes in chaos. The woman with the ketchup bottle bites the ear off the mayo guy. Another diner begins juggling soy sauce bottles while singing "Farmer in the Dell." When he drops one, he throws the other two at other patrons. One shatters on the wall by the booth next to mine, and I take cover to avoid the tiny bits of glass that rain down. A few dots of soy sauce stain my sleeve and for some reason I wonder if the sodium will be absorbed by my skin. A little girl runs to the corner and starts chewing on the leaves of the chrysanthemum tree while clawing at her neck with both hands. A man tears two sculpted golden Mandarin characters off the wall and runs out the door with them. Another cook runs out from the kitchen with a large metal bowl and screams *"Tofuuuuu tiiiime!"* at the top of his lungs, then tries stuffing handfuls of bean curd cubes into the mouths of other people.

With no obvious clear path through the melee, I slink down in my seat and attempt to hide under the table. If I can go unnoticed for a few minutes, maybe they'll all kill each other and I can escape.

And just like that, a third man bursts through the kitchen door with a roar. He has a chef's knife in each hand—in fact, they appear to be bound in place, with chrome-colored duct tape wrapped haphazardly around both fists. He swings wildly back and forth, emitting a grunt with each swipe.

The blades slice with virtually no resistance, opening necks and faces and wrists and stomachs. Bodies begin to fall, blood spurts everywhere, and the screams in the room dwindle as the diners and staff expire one by one. The floor is suddenly a patchwork of corpses in dark red puddles and disrupted platters of chicken, rice, broccoli, tofu, snow peas, and lo mein.

The man with the knives spots me beneath the table. He's at the opposite end of the dining room, which gives me a few seconds, but I have to act on instinct. I move from my knees to my feet, pressing up on the bottom of the table, launching it as far as I can in the madman's direction. Which isn't very far because it's heavier than I expected, or maybe I'm just not as strong as I thought, even with the adrenaline pumping. But at least it can act as a partial barrier, I think—an obstacle he has to navigate before reaching me.

I run for the kitchen door, thinking I can escape out the back while the knife guy climbs over the bodies and furniture in the trashed dining room. He screams at me, a babbling roar I don't recognize as being composed of any actual words.

When I push through the swinging door, I discover there's someone else back there. He doesn't say a word, but he's clearly angry. And he doesn't exactly look human anymore. His neck, shoulders, upper arms, and chest have bubbled out to an extreme degree. The size of him makes me think of some cartoon version of a professional wrestler, or a weightlifter who only works on his upper body, but expanded to a comically large size. He's so big, I don't know how his legs can even support the weight. Purple lines hatch across his neck, between rows of little yellow blisters. And the giant blisters, the bubbles deforming his upper body, pulsate independently, as if each of them is breathing on its own. There's so much bulk, he can't turn his head, and I can't understand how he can even move his arms, but he does, somehow.

He grabs both sides of a large steel refrigerator and tips it over sideways so it blocks the back door. He howls with laughter, arching his body backward slightly, the same way a werewolf would bark at the moon. So much for that idea. I'm fucked.

So now I have a decision to make, and I make it fast. No way I'm dealing with this mutant. I'll have to take my chances with the knife guy. I look around the prep tables and grab a knife of my own.

Then I take a deep breath and kick the swinging door back open toward the dining room. It catches on the treads of somebody's unmoving foot and stays open.

The knife guy is standing right there, waiting for me to reappear. His eyes are spinning and he's got a smile on his face like he's about to feast on something. I charge at him with my own blade as he swings his back and forth with both arms, sure to slice me as soon as I'm within striking distance. I should've thought through this better. But in a stroke of dumb luck, I slip on some blood and fall flat on my face well before reaching him. My knife goes flying, and lands several feet away, propping up against one of the newly deceased.

He dives in my direction, both knives coming down, but I manage to grab the one cook's wok off the ground and use it as a shield to deflect the swiping blades. The guy falls down, and from my knees, I pound him in the head three times with the wok. He's out. Maybe dead? Not sure.

I take a second to catch my breath, then stand back up. I find my knife among the bodies and the wreckage and stuff it under my belt on my hip, hoping it'll stay in place as I move about.

CRAZYTIMES

The giant in the kitchen screams like a lion and charges at me, and I tense up again, but he's mutated so large he can't fit through the doorway. He strains and pushes against the doorframe and I feel like it's going to give, but thankfully it doesn't. He seems to have trapped himself in.

I debate whether or not I should take the wok with me, but ultimately decide not to, since I think it will only draw attention my way, and that's something I definitely don't need any more of today. I have the knife to defend myself with, and if that's not enough, well . . . then maybe I don't need to make it through the day. I'm so confused, panicked, tired. I wonder where Isa is, and if she's okay. I wonder how expansive this thing is—this event, for lack of a better word. Is it a disease? Mass insanity? No, it can't just be that—there's this bizarre mutation factor, like something out of a sci-fi movie.

I hear a boom outside, the loudest one I've heard in a while. It's time to go.

I wave goodbye to the mutant in the kitchen doorway, and start for the front. He sees me go and intensifies his efforts to break through the doorframe—I can feel the room shake with his efforts, and I see a bubble on one of his shoulders explode in a mess of purple goo—but the doorframe holds. He's stuck there, maybe for good.

Good.

Then I hear a second voice groan behind me, and I turn to see the guy with the knife hands, awake again, suddenly coming at me, his eyes spinning even more wildly than before. I see one side of his neck bubble and burst outward in mid-stride, and his groan becomes a terrifying shriek of laughter as he closes in. I slide out of the way at the last second. He crashes into the front window, which makes a reverberating sound—it's thick plexi instead of real glass—and I grab two fists full of chopsticks off the table at the front of the room. I turn back toward him as he rights himself and dives at me again, still laughing, and I jam both bundles of bamboo chopsticks, still wrapped in their red paper sleeves, into his spinning eyes with a single sickening crunch. Blood spurts from the clogged holes and yellow and purple goop sputters out both sides of his mouth. His knife hands fall backward, and so does he. One last groan escapes his lips. He's finally dead.

I take another deep breath, and peek outside. It still seems calm on this block, but now that's the sort of thing that makes me nervous. I have no choice, though. I have to go.

7

WHEN I GET to the intersection at the end of the block, the world seems so much more active.

There's a lot more traffic, as if people are trying to get out of the city. Horns are blaring. People are yelling. I see smoke coming from no more than a block away, and I can smell whatever's burning. A man in mechanic's coveralls and a red, white, and blue clown wig cartwheels down the sidewalk, saying "yippee-yippee-yippee" as he goes. The sky above still has that unusual haze I noticed this morning. It's the color of rust, and I feel like the city is corroded in a way it wasn't just yesterday.

The moment I look up, something screams out of the sky at an angle—a bright, blazing thing—and crashes right into the middle of the intersection. The sound of the impact is deep, practically unbearable, and I realize the booming sounds I've been hearing since I woke up are probably the result of whatever this is.

The ground shakes as the pavement explodes open, sending chunks of rubble and dirt in all directions and knocking me off my feet. Tiny bits of gravel pummel me as I fall, and I end up choking on some of the fine debris. When the smoke and dust begin to clear, I see the impact has left a huge crater in the center of the intersection, and a pair of cars, one from each of both one-way streets, have tumbled down into the hole.

People are screaming, and I don't know if it's because they're scared or because they're crazy. I'm guessing it's a bit of both.

Someone yells "What the fuck was that?! A comet?! A meteor?! *A missile?!*"

A large woman with a bubbly neck and the familiar purple-lined pattern on it walks by calmly, pushing a baby carriage that appears to be loaded with chunks of concrete. She smiles at everyone she passes, as if they're her neighbors and she's just taking her infant out for a mid-afternoon stroll. She stops short of the intersection and leans over to pick up a sizable chunk of blacktop to add to her collection. She drops it gently into the pram and jumps up and down, announcing "I got 'em all now!", before wheeling the carriage over the edge of the crater and following it in herself, diving with perfect form, as if into a swimming pool. She screams on the way down then falls silent.

I run to the edge of the hole and spot her at the bottom among the wreckage. Her blistered neck appears to have popped—perhaps she broke it in the fall—and she's lying in a puddle of red and yellow and purple slime. Blood spurts from several parts of her twisted frame, but her neck looks the worst. She's unresponsive, but the blistered mess of her neck seems to continue pulsing.

Her collection of concrete has spilled out from the carriage, and amongst the rubble, I can see the body of a small child, flattened, bruised, and bloody. It's a heartbreaking sight on its own, but it also reminds me again of my brothers. I was there when they died, all those years ago. Although the memory of that day is somewhat foggy, I can still remember the sight of their dead bodies, and I feel guilty for being alive when their lives were cut so short.

The cars at the bottom of the crater are wrecked too, crumpled and twisted hunks of metal. There is no movement within, and I have to assume, with all I've seen, that the drivers are dead now too.

I fight the urge to puke all of a sudden, and I'm not sure why this is the first time I've felt that way today. Maybe the spring rolls were spoiled? Could they have poisoned me at the restaurant?

I see something else at the bottom of the hole too. A rock, charred black, but glowing yellow and red from within, the light visible through the valleys of the ridges on its surface. It's about the size of a bowling ball. I assume it's a meteor. Or a meteorite. Or a comet. I have no idea what the difference is. Maybe I should've paid better attention as a kid in science class.

A yellow gas hisses out of the rock in a series of short bursts. Puffs of smoke rise up above the street level, then each travels in a different direction, as if sentient, and not at all reliant on the flow of the air. I duck beneath one headed my way, though I don't know if it makes a difference.

8

ONCE I'M ABLE to escape the scene of the crash, I begin walking west, toward my part of town, and away from the river. I'm not sure why, other than the fact that subconsciously, everyone likes to be at home, whatever or wherever their "home" may be. My house hasn't felt much like home lately—not since Isa left—so I'm not sure it's that. But I also feel like staying away from the city's water supply is probably a good idea right now. Does that have anything to do with the river that flows along the eastern edge of the city, though? I have no idea. That's something else I probably should've paid more attention to in school. Regardless of where the water comes from, I decide I better not drink any unless it's bottled. Goddamn, I'm thirsty. I can still taste the hot piss from Wok Around the Clock.

I think about taking the subway west, but decide it might be best to stay above ground for the time being. Maybe. I just know I wouldn't want to be trapped inside a moving metal tube with any of these crazy people. It may not even be running anyway.

Down one street I find a series of bloody, severed nipples lying on the blood-spattered ground like a trail of breadcrumbs. I wonder where the people these nipples once belonged to could be, but decide not to follow the trail to find out.

Everywhere I go, I hear people laughing and screaming, even if I can't see them. I almost want to laugh at the absurdity of all of this myself, but I don't. I'd rather scream anyway. But I do neither and instead, just keep walking.

I pass by a guy who I think might be my friend from the coffee shop, but he's got his apron and shirt pulled up over his head, so I can't be sure. He's walking around blindly, flapping his arms like wings, and thankfully he doesn't see me. I don't stop him to say hi.

A while later, I get to the western edge of Center City. I've kept my Thousand Yard Stare the whole way, and I've seen things I never expected to encounter in my life. Things I never would have thought possible outside of old paperbacks and disaster movies.

I walk past the library, which looks like it must have been hit by a meteor. The front steps are ruined and there's a big hole with wisps of smoke pouring out where the main entrance used to be.

I think of poor Henry Bemis from *The Twilight Zone*, then remember I have his action figure in my pocket. I take him out for a second, look at Burgess Meredith's bespectacled face, and squeeze him in my fist. I'm glad I brought him along. He's my good luck charm now, and I'm going to survive as long as I can, just like he did, no matter what cruel fate awaits me. I'm glad, at least, that I don't wear glasses.

As I continue moving, I see a bus turned on its side, half in the street, half in the sidewalk, with a guy standing on top of it, bouncing up and down, screaming and raising his hands up to the sky as if he is attempting to beckon a meteor to take him out. Even at a distance, I recognize him as my bus driver from this morning, and I'm more than happy to keep my distance. His laughter echoes through the air. At least he finally stopped for something.

Soon, I've escaped Center City alive—which, when I stop to think about it, seems amazing and unlikely. Of course, technically I'm still in the city, but the west side of town is far more residential and doesn't feel like what most people would refer to as "the city." It's a little more open, with wider streets and buildings that rise no more than three stories above the ground instead of skyscrapers towering over everything.

Because the sky is more visible, I'm able to see more and more meteors—or whatever they are—sail through the air and crash to the ground. *Boom, boom, boom.* They're scattered all over the city, appearing suddenly from the rusty haze above and crashing into streets, parks, and homes. Puffs of yellow smoke float upward a minute or two after they land, and they go in various directions like before. A couple of them have crashed pretty close to me, but I've been lucky enough to avoid the smoke, not to mention a direct hit.

A pair of squirrels dash in front of me and run off into the distance. They don't scurry up any trees; it looks like they're just running as far away as they can, as quickly as they can. It occurs to me that these are the first animals I've seen all day. Normally I'll encounter at least a few dog walkers, either on my walk to the bus or outside the shop, but I don't recall seeing any today. And just like that, a guy wearing nothing but a belt and a cowboy hat appears with what looks to be a dead cat slumped over each shoulder. He runs up to a cherry blossom tree and kicks it, then screams in pain, drops the dead cats, and begins hopping up and down on his other foot. I take a hard left and pick up my pace a bit.

I pass by a supermarket and think about going in, until I see through the windows how many people are already inside, most of them attacking each other with weapons, pieces of shelves, even canned beans and cartons of milk. Most of them have that look that's become ubiquitous in just a matter of hours. I wonder if I'll escape that fate myself, if I even manage to stay alive.

I also see a number of people lying unresponsive on the linoleum floor of the market. Some appear to have bulging, purple-marked necks that still heave on their own, while others look uninfected but still dead. So as much as I want to take my chances and sneak inside to grab a jug of water, I decide it's too risky. The shelves look fairly picked over anyway, from what I'm able to see. No sense in putting myself that close to harm's way.

Seven or eight blocks later I reach Homestuff, a big-box home project superstore, and I think about the bookshelves I never got around to building at home. I wonder if my lack of follow-through on projects like that contributed to the reasons Isa left. I wouldn't be surprised. I should've been a better guy, a better partner. I guess I realize that now, although I couldn't tell you if it just dawned on me, or if it's a conclusion I've slowly been coming to over the last few months.

I wonder about her—if she's still at the bakery, or if she's at home. I don't even know where she's living these days.

I approach the store from the parking lot, scoping things out before I go inside. It looks fairly vacant, though I doubt it's empty. From what I can see through the glass door, the shelves look pretty well-stocked. It's a surprise, but a welcome one.

I imagine they've got bottled water in there. It seems like the sort of place doomsday preppers would frequent, as they ready their bunkers for the sort of day that finally came today. But I guess all the work that needed to be done before doomsday arrived was already done, and in theory all those folks are locked away underground by now. Hopefully they left some supplies behind for me. I wonder if they've been affected in their bunkers anyway, if they've mutated, if they're tearing each other apart underground.

The Homestuff door has a sensor, and slides open when I get close enough to trigger it. It emits a low chime as it opens, and I freeze one step in on the concrete floor to see if the sound summons anyone. It doesn't, and I'm thankful.

I move cautiously down one aisle, then another, and find no one, which is nearly as shocking as anything else I've seen today, but I won't waste time sweating it. I look up too—this is one of those stores that's essentially a huge warehouse, with metal shelving units rising what must be thirty or forty feet up, packed with boxes and planks of wood and every diameter of PVC piping you could possibly need. I keep thinking someone's going to jump out at me from behind a water heater, or from inside a display model of a refrigerator. It doesn't happen, though.

I find a small section offering a few different kinds of backpacks, and grab a canvas one off the wall. I also find some elbow and kneepads—the kind roofers use, I think. And there's a sporting goods section, where I find a chest protector that seems light enough, and even if it's only fabric and stuffing, it looks like it'll offer some level of protection. I think maybe a helmet would be a good idea too, but I don't see any.

Then I discover cases of bottled water, miraculously untouched. I tear into the outer plastic casing, still trying to remain quiet, and twist the cap off a bottle. I chug it down in a matter of seconds, realizing water has never tasted so good, then set the empty down on a shelf, and pour half of another down my throat. I toss eight or nine more bottles into the backpack, and figure that's about all I can carry with relative ease, then I slide a few cases of water deeper into the back of the shelf they're on, and move some other items in front of them, to keep them hidden. Who knows—I may need to come back here later and get more.

Somewhere in the process, I realize the knife I had taken from the Chinese restaurant is no longer with me. I remember thinking I might lose it when I tucked it into my belt, and then I wonder why I didn't just secure it better. Knife-wielding rookie mistake, I guess. I wonder where I could have lost it, but realize there's no sense in trying to figure it out. It's not like I'm going to retrace my steps and go back into the madness downtown.

So I have one more thing to shop for, apparently. I need something sharp.

9

OF COURSE THE thing I'm looking for would be at the very back of this massive store. I'm still amazed at how utterly devoid of people it is. This place probably has everything one could need in an end-of-the-world scenario, except maybe food. Although there are some snacks in one of the aisles. Mostly trail mix. About fifty varieties of trail mix. And a few energy drinks. But my heart is thumping just fine, thank you very much.

That is what we're dealing with here, isn't it? The end of the world. Sure feels like it. But who knows. I feel like there's nothing I can be completely sure of right now.

Could I hole up in here? Seems like it could be safe. Maybe.

No. Way too much space to defend. Too many directions for others to come from and too few paths to take if I'm caught halfway down an aisle. And way too many things for crazies to grab and use as weapons.

And should the cavalry come rolling into town, would they

even find me deep within the bowels of this gigantic place? Better to get what I need and find somewhere else cozy to barricade myself in.

Along the back-most aisle, I see what I need. Knives. Hand scythes. Machetes. Perfect. I suppose I could grab some firearms just as easily, but I wouldn't know what the hell I was doing with them. I'd likely shoot myself in the foot, either figuratively or literally. Plus, who wants to carry ammo around? Ammo that makes loud noises and calls attention to itself. And also runs out. Plus, guns jam. From what I've read, at least. Never happens in action movies, of course, but that would probably be my luck.

I might as well stick with something I know how to use. Sharp things. I can stab and chop with the best of 'em. I've already done it today, I feel like I've got the experience I need, and I'm prepared to do it again.

As I approach the back wall with the knife display, I hear something. It's the smallest sound, but I'm hyper-sensitive to my surroundings right now. I jump back into one of the aisles and crouch down behind a giant cardboard box, and I hear the noise again. It's a soft sound, but it repeats. Footsteps. Careful footsteps. It's someone approaching as quietly as they can, trying to sneak up on me. But they're not quiet enough.

I wasn't able to grab a knife before ducking away, so I've got to rely on my hands and feet to defend myself. Maybe I can heave the backpack at my attacker.

This other person—it sounds like just one person—is in the next aisle over. The shelves are packed full, so I can't see through to scope out what they look like, but I brace myself. I stand a little taller and get ready to pounce the moment they round the corner, and suddenly there's movement and I jump out. I swing the loaded backpack around from behind me, both hands on the top strap, but I pull up at the last second and smash the pack into the endcap of the aisle instead.

"Holy shit!"

It's Jenny. The white rims of her glasses look scuffed and dirty, and she no longer has her hat, but otherwise she looks good.

"Trey!" she gasps, then takes a deep breath. "Oh man, I thought I was dead there for a second."

I take a moment to catch my breath too. She reaches out toward me and we hug, both happy to find another survivor with their wits about them.

"You're alone?" I say.

"Yeah, I decided to head out this way when shit started getting crazy downtown. I went to the falafel cart a couple blocks over and this dude started swinging fists, so I ran. Then I went to the deli instead, but the people there were just talking gibberish to each other, like it was normal, and drooling when I tried to order—like, literally drooling all over the counter, and laughing like a bunch of loons—so I bailed on that idea too. Eventually I went back to the shop and saw all the blood. I figured you were dead too." She pauses and huffs. "Glad you're not. What the fuck is going on?"

I wish I had an answer for her. She's seen the meteors too,

CRAZYTIMES

so we both know that much. We talk about the yellow smoke and the purple marks and the crazy laughter and the bulging mutated bubbling flesh, but that's all the info we have.

"I mean, why would these meteors turn some people into crazy killers, and make other people just regular boring-crazy, and meanwhile you and I are fine?" she says.

"I don't know. Isa used to think people were slowly going crazy already. She used to say it was something in the water."

Jenny bobs her eyebrows and tilts her head to one side, as if to say the idea sounds reasonable. "So maybe regular crazy is from the water and killer crazy is from the meteors?"

"Could be. And maybe some of us have a natural genetic defense against whatever this shit is." I start looking through the store's selection of knives and other sharp tools. The hand scythes look really fucking cool, but I'm not sure how practical a curved weapon like that is going to be in close proximity. "Who knows what kind of germs are out there, in the water, or out in space. Ya know? Not everybody gets the flu every year, right?"

"True," she agrees. "Some people never get chicken pox their entire lives."

"Who the hell knows. Maybe the meteors aren't the cause of it anyway. Maybe they're another result." But I abandon the thought there. We have no way of knowing what's happening. We're not scientists. We don't have any data. This is all just speculation.

I start examining the machetes and begin thinking maybe that's the way to go. An eighteen-inch blade is plenty sharp, and long enough to keep someone a safe distance away. Suddenly I remember the look on Kia's face back at the shop when she was swinging the guillotine blade around, and I shudder. It's an image I hope to block out completely one day. For now, though, I feel like I ought to keep it in my mind. It'll help keep me alert, and hopefully keep me alive.

Jenny starts going through a display case full of knives and building up a pile of the ones she likes. None of them look like they weigh too much, so I guess it can't hurt to stock up. Maybe I'll grab a few for myself. But I'm keeping a machete as my primary weapon. It just feels right. I tie the sheath onto my leg at first, then realize having it strapped to my back might offer a quicker retrieval of the blade, so I do that. I have to take the chest protector off first, then I tie on the machete and slide my backpack on over it.

"Did you see these?" I ask, turning to model the pack. "They're in aisle three or four, I think. Want me to grab you one?"

"Oh, yeah, that would be great," she says. "Then I guess we oughta roll, huh?"

I agree. It can't be too much longer before someone else shows up here, and the likelihood of them being friendly seems pretty low.

"I have a place in mind that might be safe," she says as I move farther away. I pretend I don't hear her, though. I'd rather we not start screaming to each other across the store. There's still a chance someone could be lurking nearby.

I move up and down aisles three and four, then aisle five, and finally I find the backpack display. In aisle six. Apparently I had grabbed the last one in this particular style, but I find another one that's similar, with plenty of compartments, and it seems like a good choice.

I head back toward Jenny and the knives, but decide to make a short detour on the way and load her bag with some packages of trail mix and a couple bottles of water.

I hear a clatter a second before I reach the back aisle again. Sounds like Jenny dropped a knife on the floor or something. Then I turn the corner.

"Jenny? What are you—"

She's standing there on one leg, her opposite foot pressed against the inside of her thigh. A yoga position? Except she's juggling knives.

"Sorry," she says. "Just dropped one."

It takes a second, but I realize there are a few drops of blood on the concrete floor in front of her, in addition to the fallen knife.

"Are you okay?"

She's juggling the knives by their exposed blades, with each touch slicing into the skin of her fingers and palms. She doesn't react to it. It's as if she doesn't feel the cuts, but flecks of blood are starting to fly all over as she continues.

"Check it out," she screams in a terrible attempt at a British accent. *"I'm a bloody jugglah!"* Then she starts laughing.

It only takes another second for me to notice the purple

crisscrossed lines on her neck. Were they there before, hidden by her hair? Or did they just appear now? She seemed normal when we first ran into each other, I didn't even think to examine her. Her eyes weren't spinning then, but they are now.

She must have inhaled some of that meteor gas at some point. But when? I wonder how long it takes for the reaction to set in.

She tosses all the knives up in the air at once and spreads her arms wide, yelling "Ta-da!" and showing me her blood-drenched, sliced-up hands. The blades cascade down around her like rain. The butt of one hits her shoulder but she doesn't seem to notice. Then she reaches up to scratch her neck, smearing the purple lines with red. She continues to laugh emphatically, and won't stop.

Oh Jenny. Not you too. I think I say it out loud, but I'm not sure. It doesn't matter. It doesn't stop her from suddenly turning violent in the midst of her maniacal laughter, and she begins picking knives up off the ground to throw at me.

Luckily she has terrible aim and nothing hits me. She keeps trying, but I guess since her eyes are spinning in circles, she probably doesn't see much more than blurs of light and shadow. I hold the extra backpack up in front of me to block anything that comes close. When she runs out of the knives she had chosen from the display, she goes right back over to it to get some more.

Her head cocks to one side suddenly, and even from behind, beneath her long hair, I can see the flesh of her neck and shoulder begin to bulge, bursting outward like a series of small bags inflating in rapid succession.

I consider charging at her, but my legs freeze up, as if they're second-guessing the thought.

She turns back toward me, and her aim has improved. Knife after knife sails in my direction, and I use the backpack to knock away the ones I can't dodge. I think about running, but even if I get away from her, she'll still be around to hurt others. Or kill others. I have to take care of her.

I lead with the backpack shield held up high and pull the machete from the sheath on my back as I dart toward her. She only has time to throw one more at me, and I manage to knock it to the side as I dive at her, bringing the long blade down onto her shoulder. She screams, although I'm not sure it's from pain. Blood sprays and yellow ooze leaks from the wound, and I see I've nearly taken her arm off with one swipe. The machete is lodged inside her shoulder now, though, and I can't seem to extract it with any ease. She looks down at the wound and laughs, spitting, like it's the most hilarious thing she's seen in a week.

I press forward and we crash into one of the display cases. Glass shatters down on both of us. Jenny grabs a knife from the case with her good hand and swings it around behind me. I feel something wet run down my back almost instantly and I think she's gotten me, then I realize she's just stabbed into one of the water bottles inside my pack.

I can't pull the machete loose so I let go, take a step back, and grab the wrist of her wounded arm with both hands. Without thinking, I tug violently, then raise a leg and place my foot against her sternum. I push and pull and the machete falls, clanging to the floor as her arm separates from her body. I've still got both hands around her wrist, and I beat her repeatedly in the face with her own severed arm, using it like a club. Blood spatters everywhere, dotting the display cases and the shelves and the floor, and I don't stop until her laughter stops and finally she's lying still.

10

ONCE I'VE GATHERED a few knives and swapped my backpack for one without a hole, I'm out the door. I grab a few extra bottles of water too, because I'm not sure when I might be headed back here after all.

If I run into someone, I wonder what the best course of action should be. Do I keep a low profile and try to pass unnoticed? Or do I act extra-crazy in the hopes that even the crazy ones will avoid me? Or do I destroy everybody and everything in my way? As the hours pass, it seems more and more like it's the end of the world, and kill or be killed is the code to live by.

I take River Road, which oddly enough, runs alongside a train line instead of a river. For some reason I feel like that might be less inhabited than other streets, and once I'm there, it seems like a good decision. It's not completely vacant, but there aren't too many people, and most of them are far enough away that I have plenty of time to alter my route and avoid them if I want.

I have to step over numerous body parts along the way—several arms, including one without a hand, a leg still wrapped in the fabric of its pants leg, a couple ears, a head missing one ear, and something I initially think is a child's arm but quickly realize is an uncircumcised penis.

The farther I walk, the more trees there are separating the train tracks from the street, so I duck into the wooded area to keep cover. There's smoke above, which makes me think some meteors must have crashed nearby, although it could easily be a car engulfed in flames. I grabbed a pack of surgical masks on my way out of the superstore too. I tear into the package and put one on, wondering if it's even going to help. Can't hurt, I suppose.

The road curves and diverges from the train line, and in the space between, the trees eventually diminish and the land opens up into a field with benches around the perimeter. A park. I'm not too far from my house at this point, and yet I've never been to this place. It looks kind of nice, actually, and I wonder why I never took advantage. Would've been a nice place to sit and read.

I see some kids—three boys, it looks like, no older than eight or nine—running around up ahead, kicking a soccer ball and laughing and yelling. They aren't the sounds of anger, though. They seem to just be having fun. I feel the hint of a smile crawl across my lips, and for a moment I hope and think maybe things are going to be okay. I imagine how nice it would have been if I'd had the chance to play soccer with my brothers like these boys.

My thought gets interrupted by a large man emerging from another wooded area at the far end of the field. He's much closer to the boys, and he begins running toward them. The boys abandon their ball and run off screaming. The fear is real, but at least they're smart enough to go in three different directions. At least, I hope that's the right move and they're able to reconvene elsewhere. Getting stuck on your own during the apocalypse is not something I would recommend.

The man is clearly insane, shouting a series of non-words and animalistic yelps. Even from this distance I can see the purple marks and the misshapen quality of his neck. Confused by the scattering, he pauses for a moment before chasing after one of the children. He appears to choose correctly, as the boy he follows isn't a particularly good runner. The man catches up to him quickly and tackles him to the ground. Then he stands back up, grabs the boy by his ankles, and beats him against the ground like a doll, laughing all the while. He whips the child over and over against the grass, and for a moment I liken the motion to someone trying to work the kinks out of a hose, but this is far messier.

I start running toward the altercation, but I'm too far away to make a difference. The boy has the wind knocked out of him right away, and his body quickly falls limp and lifeless into the now-flattened grass.

The man notices me coming, though, and as soon as the boy

has been dispatched, he turns his gaze toward me. I stop dead in my tracks, just as he starts walking in my direction with purpose. A few steps in, he breaks into a run.

Even from a distance, even as he bounds toward me, I can see his neck pulsating. Yellow and purple goop spatters from his mouth as he shouts malformed sounds in an accusatory way. I see his eyes spinning too, like I've seen far too many times today.

I'm ready for him, though. I angle my stance sideways and slide the machete from the sheath on my back, then I wait while he expends the bulk of the effort. He's coming fast in the last fifty feet or so. Thirty. Twenty. Ten. Five.

At the last moment, I slide one step over and swing the machete right to left. It's not like Jenny. It doesn't get stuck. Aided by his momentum, it's one clean movement and his head hits the ground and rolls a lumpy path about twenty feet or so, spitting multicolored goo the whole way, before stopping in a patch of dead grass.

His arms swipe wildly out in front of him, and one of his fingers catches the corner of my surgical mask, snapping it free from my face. So much for that.

The rest of his body falls to its knees, then slams chest-first into the ground. Red and yellow liquid pours from his neck stump, like milk heaving out of a dropped plastic jug.

I pause for a moment, feeling like a samurai warrior, then I wipe both sides of my blade on the guy's pant leg and replace it in its sheath.

For a second I think about running up and booting his head

like a soccer ball, but I reconsider before acting on the urge, and move along.

I walk over to the lifeless child's body and pay my respects. What the point of that is, I'm not sure, but I've got my brothers on my mind, and this kid is another reminder of a promise cut short. I didn't know him, but his tragic circumstances have some weight, and I'm feeling it. My eyes well up, and a few tears fall from my cheeks.

I approach the soccer ball the kids were playing with a minute later. I wonder if the other two will ever come back for it, come back and find their friend lying dead in the grass. If they survive themselves. Hopefully they haven't been attacked already. Hopefully they don't go crazy like so many others. Hopefully they make it through the day and find somewhere safe to lay their heads tonight.

When I get close enough to the ball, my jaw drops. It's not a soccer ball. It's a meteor.

11

I'M HESITANT TO get too close, but the meteor appears to be inert. It's just lying there, doing nothing. It's not glowing. It doesn't seem to be radiating any heat. It's charred, but there is no smoke rising up from between its ridges. The kids were kicking it around like it was nothing. Maybe it's already spat out its toxins and it's nothing but a spent shell now.

Fuck. What do I do?

I decide to do the thing people always do in sci-fi movies. I find a long stick and use it to poke the meteor. The thing has some weight to it, but it's light enough that when I touch it with the end of the branch, it moves. It's relatively round, but has an uneven, rocky surface, scorched black from its journey through the atmosphere.

The last one of these I saw up close was downtown, a few hours ago, and it glowed from within, bright red and yellow, like it had a miniature furnace inside.

CRAZYTIMES

And it's as if the thought conjures something into reality. Suddenly a red dot appears from within the meteor. I stagger back, startled by what I'm seeing, and I think for a second that it's really all over now and maybe that's okay because I lasted longer than most. I wait for the yellow puff of smoke to appear and take me, absolving me of that irritating sense of survivor's guilt I've always carried with me, but it doesn't come.

Then for some reason I take a step toward the meteor and realize the little spot of red is a light. Not a fiery glow, but an actual electronic light, like a tiny LED. It's blinking, pulsing like a slow heartbeat. It does this for a full minute while I watch, riveted, unsure of what to expect next, but hanging on the moment. Then the light disappears for several seconds, only to reappear, this time bright blue and solid.

The meteor beeps. One loud, solid tone.

I tense up further, not expecting this at all. I brace myself. I think perhaps it's a bomb, about to explode, but instead, two sections of the rocklike sphere slide out from opposite sides and right the shape into a specific, steady position. It beeps again, this time softer, and from beneath the two extended sections, a pair of tiny blue fires ignite. They appear to be twin rocket boosters, and the thing, clearly not a meteor, but instead some sort of device, launches itself up into the air, propelling itself higher and higher, only to disappear into the hazy sky, which I only now realize is darkening quickly.

Fuck.

I stand there in total disbelief. As if *any* of the things that have happened today could be believed on any other day.

I need to move, but my legs don't want to. It's a sensation I'm getting sick of feeling.

I look up, then across the horizon, and back toward Center City. It looks like war, like bombs being dropped from drones flying high above, while missiles are sent up to counter the threat. Only I don't think we're fighting whatever is happening. I think the things going up in the sky are just the things that came down, and they're going back up through the clouds for reinforcements.

Where the hell is our military anyway? Shouldn't the sky be filled with fighter jets? Shouldn't tanks be firing at the meteors, disintegrating them before they ever have a chance to crash and spread their madness? Maybe the generals have gone crazy, and the soldiers have run away. Maybe they've got their own bunkers to hide in, realizing we have no chance against whatever this is.

So maybe this *whatever* is even bigger than I thought. If I wasn't convinced already, I have to assume this is happening all over, not just here. The question is, where's it coming from? And what's the reason? Or does any of that even matter?

Oh, it's a playground. It's not a park. The thought blindsides me. There are bigger issues afoot, but this is the thing that jolts me back into action. I must have gotten turned around at some point, gotten confused about where I was walking. Of course. On the other side of those trees is the Alexandria School. K through 5. How could I have forgotten? Isa and I had once talked about how, if we ever had kids together, they would probably go to school here one day.

Only I didn't want kids. Which was probably another reason she bailed. Not that I was ever really given reasons, so I just have to speculate, like I've been doing with the crazy people and the meteors and everything else.

The sky gets noticeably darker in a matter of moments, and I realize I better find somewhere safe to hide out, at least for the night. If I'm still around tomorrow when the sun returns, maybe I can do some more scavenging for supplies, but for now I better get inside.

I start jogging across the field and through the trees, to the parking lot for the school, thinking there has to be a classroom or an office I can barricade myself inside. Surely the doors have locks, and if not, I could always stack up a bunch of desks and chairs.

As I walk along the edge of the parking lot and reach the corner of the building, I hear the laughter of children. *Lots* of children. And I hear a man screaming.

12

"COME ON, WE need to get you inside!" the man says. He's upset, but maybe not the kind of angry I'm thinking he might be at first. Mostly, he sounds urgent. "Please, let's get inside the school."

I hear the sounds of children clamoring too, but they're a little more distant, and I don't think he's talking to them. When I peek around the corner of the building, I see them at the opposite end of the U-shaped school, inside, laughing and slapping their hands on the windows. They're not coming out, though, which makes me think they're stuck in whatever room that is.

"Why can't I just stay right here?" It's a woman responding. "I can sleep on this bench," she pleads. She sounds utterly exhausted. She sounds familiar.

"It's like twenty feet to the door," the guy says. I step away from the corner of the building and hide behind a lone tree where I have a better view of things. I see him standing in front of her, holding her hand. She's seated with one leg up on the bench and the other on the ground. The bench sits on an angle along the edge of the walkway that leads to the main doors to the school, located in the concave center of the U. I can't see her face or her body, but it's clear from the sound of her voice that she's spent.

"Let's just get inside," the guy continues. "I'll find some pillows or something. They've gotta have a bed in the nurse's office, right? It'll be so much more comfortable than this bench. You can sleep, and I'll scrounge up some food, and everything will be alright."

"Okay," she relents, sitting up straighter with a deep sigh. She seems to be gathering her energy. "Fine. Let's go. Help me up?"

The guy bends at the knees, grabs her other hand, and pulls, helping her to her feet. When he moves to the side, I see why she sounds so familiar. She used to live with me.

Of all the people to run into at the end of the world.

Isa winces as she turns toward the door, stifling a scream. She's in obvious pain. She grabs her belly.

Fuck.

She's pregnant? Fuck, fuck, fuck.

I had no idea. That must have been yet another reason she left. Not that we were getting along anyway, but she knew how badly I didn't want children. She obviously knew before she moved out, but wasn't showing yet. Or if she was, I sure didn't notice. It's not like we had been exploring each other's bodies much those last few months. *How far along is she now?* I wonder. She looks big.

Wait, am I even the father? Maybe. Maybe not. It could just as easily be this guy with her. By the looks of things, she's got to be at least seven or eight months along. I try to remember how long ago the last time we had sex was. Could she have been cheating while we were together?

Does it really matter right now anyway?

I almost call her name, but decide against it, and stay where I am behind the tree. It's the only cover I have for the moment. There's the tree and the bench, and a shrub behind it. Everything else right here is flat and paved.

The children in the far windows get more animated when Isa stands up and she and her companion turn toward the door to the school. Their voices get much louder, although I can't tell what they're screaming. But the sound of them pounding against the windows and walls is intense. Sounds like thunder. Like an approaching storm.

For a second, I think *Oh no, they're trapped*, but I quickly realize that's not the case. It only takes one kid to convince me, with his face pressed against the glass, smiling wide while he licks a circle of grime clean from the windowpane.

Isa and the guy only make it a few steps away from the bench before she's hit with a shock of pain. She grabs the underside of her round belly, groans loudly, and falls to one knee.

"I can't," she says between labored breaths. "I . . . I can't."

"Come on, we're almost there." He has her arm just above

the elbow and tries to help her stand again.

She winces, then screams. She can't take the pain. I want to help, but don't know how I can, or if she'd even want me to.

She screams again. Agony. She lurches forward as if something hit her from behind. But it didn't.

"Isa!" I yell, finally stepping out from behind the tree, and she turns around, eyes wide, and falls on her butt, startled. The guy turns to look in my direction too, and takes a defensive stance, as if I'm about to attack them, but I'm so focused on Isa I don't even see his face. I raise my hands in a gesture of peace, but before I'm able to take a step toward them, Isa screams again, and something in her belly pops outward suddenly, puffing her unfamiliar pastel flower-print dress out and instantly staining it red.

Blood spatters the guy's pants leg, and they both scream, terrified and confused. Isa's stomach erupts in a series of violent up and down motions beneath the fabric of her dress until finally it splits and the thing inside her breaks free from within, in a geyser of blood and pus. I can see her eyes roll back as she collapses backward immediately, the back of her head thumping on the paved walkway, and when the baby emerges through her split belly, it's a monstrous thing, slicked red. Even through the coating of blood and slime, I can make out the purple pattern on its neck and the bulging contours of its tiny mutated form.

It moves with more strength and more purpose than a newborn, though. Is that the right way to refer to this thing? This crazed mutant child with its pulsating bubbles of flesh?

I watch in horror as it pulls its feet from the vile hole in Isa's midsection, then crawls across her and somehow has the strength to snap the umbilical cord and leap from Isa onto the man's legs, latching onto the loose material of his pants, and crawl quickly up the front of him, before sinking its jagged gums into his neck. This thing has far more strength than it should. Isa's friend screams and flails, trying to shake the mutant baby off, but it seems to have intensely strong jaws, and he's unsuccessful. In mere seconds, the child tears a chunk of flesh free from the man's neck and his wild motions stop and he falls dead in a heap on top of Isa's lifeless body.

The baby-thing jumps down off him, then turns and gallops at me like an angry red dog. A glop of gore falls out of its mouth as it dives at me, leaping from all fours. I'm able to dodge it, then I spin around and nearly trip over Isa's leg. I catch myself from falling, though. Then the thing leaps at me again, and without even thinking, I grab my machete and hold it straight out in front of me like a spear. I impale the mutant child right through its evil little heart, and its momentum carries it up and over. I launch it backwards over my head like a shovelful of dirt and the little body hits the paved walkway with a wet thud. I run over to it quickly and drive the blade straight down into its mutated chest, and it stops moving for good.

That was easier than I expected.

But of course this is the moment I hear the shattering of glass, and sounds of all the purple-necked, laughing schoolchildren finally breaking free from the far end of the school.

13

I WANT TO take a moment to mourn Isa in her presence, but the kids are coming fast, and I have no choice but to run. I could try to fight them off with my blades, but there are so many, I'm sure to be overwhelmed.

This disaster movie keeps getting worse.

I run. I don't even know where I find the energy, but I run and run and run. The kids follow, but thankfully their legs are only so long, which gives me an advantage. I look back and see some of them with rulers and pencils in their hands, brandishing them like knives. One particularly menacing-looking child has a giant T-square that he's holding with both hands like a pick-axe. It looks wet. Every one of them is either screaming or laughing. Before we get out of the parking lot, the lampposts illuminate them enough for me to see the blisters on their necks and the purple goo drooling out of their mouths. Some of them look truly deformed, with massive clusters of bubbles rising up out of the skin of their necks and shoulders and backs. It's a terrifying sight, multiplied by at least a hundred.

Occasionally one or two of them sprints forward and catches up to me, and I have to dispatch them on the run. I'm surprised at how good I've gotten swinging the machete while moving.

As I run, I have to navigate puddles of blood and slime, and hurdle the bodies of the newly deceased. I jump over one of our clients from work—a guy who used to get business cards every few months for his window-washing business. He's easy to recognize because he's wearing the same obnoxiously bright orange hat and t-shirt he always wore, to stand out and bring attention to his business. They practically glow. He used to say he'd be working 'til his dying day, and it looks like he was right.

It's past dusk now, fully dark, and yet I have no trouble seeing the path ahead. Somehow the power grid is still up and streetlamps are working. Plus, the meteor-things continue to crash all around, temporarily lighting up the sky with their descending fire.

I wonder what the odds are that I haven't been hit by one of them yet.

And just like that, a meteor crashes right behind me, cratering the ground and taking out most of the kids on my tail. *What a bizarre stroke of luck*, I think. I've never been so thankful for an apocalyptic meteor that may actually be some kind of toxic gas-emitting spacecraft to hit the ground by my feet and kill a bunch of children.

CRAZYTIMES

What a day.

Eventually my pace slows to a jog, and then I stop. My legs are jelly, and I'm not sure how I'm still standing on them. I almost fall to the ground, but I realize there are still a handful of children coming after me, including that maniac with the T-square. Obviously they've gotten tired too, though. I wait for each of them to catch up to me, one by one, and I chop them down. It's easy. I never thought I'd say that about decapitating children, regardless of my feelings about parenthood, but things have changed significantly since I woke up this morning.

The meteors slow down considerably too. In a matter of minutes they stop completely, and the sky goes totally dark. I can't even see the stars.

But I continue moving. Because I have to. I mean, as long as I want to stay alive.

Do I?

When the smoke clears—if it clears—what kind of world is going to be left? Do I really want to live in it? And even if I do, what makes me so special? Why should I be one of the lucky survivors? Again.

This guilt again. Why was I the one who survived? What did I do that was so special? I was a child. But so were they. And I lived and they died.

I ponder this as I walk alongside some tall iron fencing—the posts terminate in spikes along the top—and chug a bottle of water, then toss the bottle back over my shoulder. Recycling probably bought us some time, but unfortunately it didn't save the world.

Under a flickering yellow streetlight, I find the gate. It's locked with a length of chain and a padlock, but there's enough slack that it's still able to swing partially open, and I'm able to squeeze through with a bit of effort.

I realize where I am pretty quickly, when I stub my toe on something made of stone.

This is Western Cemetery, and . . . *holy shit, you've got to be kidding me.*

14

ZOMBIES. ARE YOU fucking serious? This day has been the greatest fucking cosmic joke ever, and now there are fucking zombies? Because of course there are fucking zombies. Why the hell not?

Right in the middle of the graveyard, there's a huge crater with a dull glow coming from the bottom. The clouds of smoke drifting up from it are yellow—there's enough light from the malfunctioning streetlamps to see that—and just like usual, they drift in various directions, as if they have instructions to visit a dozen different destinations.

Does this toxic shit raise the dead too? And if so, how?

I've never really understood how zombies were supposed to work anyway. At least, not the ones coming out of the ground. The freshly expired, sure—I could see that. But once a body's been scraped out and embalmed, stuffed with a mess of detached and deflated organs, and sawdust and rags and whatever else, how is that supposed to work? It's just a shell of a human, like a handful of spoiled fruit salad with an orange peel wrapped around it.

Okay, bad analogy. But still.

It doesn't change the fact I'm suddenly surrounded by reanimated corpses, moaning and stumbling around the cemetery. Unless it's all just one big joke.

Because this has to be a joke, right? What else could explain it? It doesn't make any sense.

Whatever this is, whatever is making people crazy, whatever's making them kill, it's just a joke. If you don't laugh at it all, maybe you'll go crazy yourself.

I think of Henry Bemis and his circumstances. All alone in the world, he finally had a chance to read all the books he wanted—until his glasses broke.

I reach into my pocket for the action figure. I want to give my good luck charm a squeeze, but my hand goes right into my pocket and out the hole at the bottom. I look down and find a slash across my pants leg. When did that happen? Thinking back, I guess it could've been one of those crazed schoolkids swiping at me, though I could have just as easily snagged my pocket somewhere, like on the cemetery gate I squeezed through. Thankfully I'm not cut—it's just my pants—but my good luck charm's gone now, and I hope that's not a bad omen.

A man in a filthy suit approaches from my left, slowly, hunched over, his arms hanging slack. His withered legs look as if they can barely support the rest of him. His cheeks are sunken and his eyes are closed. He's moaning as if in pain, but his mouth stays shut. When he gets close enough I can see the stitches on his eyelids and lips.

What I don't see, however, are those purple markings I've been seeing on the living. There are no yellow blisters. There is no mutating bubbling flesh. In fact, there's not much flesh at all.

Still, the man comes at me, shambling. He bumps into a tombstone, which alters his course slightly, and causes some dirt to fall off his jacket, then he rights himself. Even though he obviously can't see much—how could his eyes possibly work anyway, even if they weren't sewn shut?—he seems to know exactly where I'm standing.

Does he want to eat my flesh? Does he even have the strength to tear his own lips apart?

I hold still and keep quiet, to conserve the tiniest bit of energy, then when he gets close enough, I stab him right through the chest with my machete. I'm surprised how easily it goes in.

I'm also surprised how quickly I've forgotten the rules of zombie lore. You gotta kill the brain. *The brain that's already dead?*

I tug at the machete, but it's stuck. I tug again. Why does this keep happening? Must be caught on a rib or something. He swipes at me with one hand, catching the fabric of my shirt on a ragged fingernail. Then I back up a few steps and drop my backpack to the ground, retrieve a knife, and stab the guy right through the eye, trying to make sure I angle upward enough that it breaks through the top of the orbital bone and pierces the brain. I guess I'm successful, because he stops sludging toward me right away and falls face-first to the ground, and the butt of the knife taps and slides against a tombstone. The gust of wind from his body falling reeks of wet earth and burnt rubber.

I roll the guy over with my foot, surprised at how light he is, and extract the knife from his face. The machete is still stuck in his chest, but with a little bit of wriggling, I'm able to remove it. And just in time too, since a pair of zombie women are suddenly approaching from the opposite direction. One is significantly smaller than the other, which makes me think of them as mother and daughter, even though I'm sure that's not the case.

I swipe at the first woman—the mom—with my machete, swinging sideways at her head. I envision the blade going right through, the top of her head popping off like something in a cartoon, but again it gets stuck partway in. It's easy enough to dislodge this time, though, and it went far enough in that she drops. I'm gonna have to figure out a way to get this thing sharpened. Next hardware store I see, I better grab a stone and some oil. Don't think I'll be backtracking to Homestuff anytime soon.

With the daughter, I decide to stab into her eye, like I did with the first guy, but using the machete from a slightly greater distance instead. Success.

I have to say, one nice thing about killing zombies is no blood. They're all dried up, so it's just a little bit of dirt and the occasional worm. Not exactly what you see in the movies.

Much like in the movies, however, they keep coming. I kill one off, then three more appear behind it. I wonder if it's some latent instinct that still exists in the brain or the body or whatever that makes them chase after the living. No, that doesn't make any sense. I don't know.

I'm kind of enjoying their easy dispatch, though. It's almost like a video game on the easiest level, hacking and slicing through a bunch of enemies who don't put up too much of a fight.

But I'm being dumb. What I really need to be doing is finding some food and finally getting tucked away inside some sort of shelter. I could keep slashing zombies, sure, but it's not like I'm facing an immediate threat. I can outrun them easily. Hell, I can *outwalk* these husks. So I pick my bag up and slide right back out the gate I came in.

15

I JOG FOR about ten minutes and at that point the zombies are so far behind, I can't see them ever catching up, if they even have the inclination and aren't distracted by something else, so I slow to a walking pace. A fresh wave of adrenaline has helped push me to this point, but I know I'll need to eat something soon. And sleep. I desperately need sleep.

Somehow I've forgotten all about the trail mix in my bag until now, so I fish a package out and crunch down on some nuts and seeds and dried fruit, but I realize it's only going to last me so long. I need to focus on finding a place where I can lay my head down for a few hours, but my second priority is going to be searching for more food.

The area I'm walking through is primarily residential, similar to my own neighborhood, though I've gotten way off track and am no longer anywhere close to my house. Maybe I'll head back over that way tomorrow. At this point, though, I just need some sleep.

I come to a church on the corner of a big intersection. It's an old place, made of stone, big but not mammoth. It looks bigger than it is, actually, because it's up on a hill. There are a bunch of steps to climb before you can get inside. Seems like a fairly exclusive thing for a place that's supposed to be so loving, but whatever.

I remember seeing this church on the news about a year ago when the bell tower collapsed. The rubble is still lying there, and I wonder why it was never cleaned up. Maybe they didn't have the money? There's caution tape and big orange construction barriers around that side of the building, though, so I guess they were getting around to it. Then again, visible ruins are certainly a strong way to appeal for donations.

Anyway, I feel like this might be a good place to hole up, despite the collapsed portion. Something about it is calling to me, and although I've never been a religious guy, I decide to follow the feeling. What could possibly go wrong that I haven't yet encountered today anyway?

I circle the perimeter of the building before going in, just to make sure there's no imminent threat waiting to corner me the second I approach one of the doors. Thankfully I don't encounter anyone.

I find the door farthest from the ruins and panic for a moment, thinking what if I can't get in? What if it's locked? Then I try the door and realize I'm being paranoid. Can you blame me?

The old wooden door opens an inch, then sticks, so I have

to use my shoulder. When it moves, the iron hinges creak under the weight of it. They don't make 'em like this anymore. The sound makes me freshly nervous, and I pause for a second to make sure I haven't roused anyone hiding out inside.

It's dark as hell in here, I think, then chuckle at my bad pun. If there's a demon priest inside, I'm gonna lose it, but I'll be ready to send him back where he came from.

I should've grabbed a flashlight back at Homestuff, or at least some candles and matches. The thought never occurred to me. Dumb.

When I move inside, I can barely see. It takes a minute, but soon my eyes adjust to the light. I enter the sanctuary from the side and realize I'm up near the altar. I see a trio of three-digit numbers on a placard—hymns from the last service held here.

I wonder when that was, and if it will be the last service ever. Maybe.

As I turn the corner, I see a dim glow coming from up front, dancing on the stone walls. My first thought is that somehow a meteor crashed through the stained glass, landing inside the church. Maybe this is a different church than the one I was thinking of, and the meteor took out the tower on its way into the building. But no—the stained glass looks intact from what I can tell.

As I approach the glow, which is maybe another dumb move, I see what it is. A single red candle with a flickering flame, right up on the altar.

I scan the room to see who else is here, but I see no evidence of life beyond the candle. Even if someone had just arrived, I would expect to see some supplies, maybe a bag or some blankets or something. But no.

I step up onto the altar and look around, then I move back down and walk among the pews. There is no evidence of anyone. No crazy people. No mutant people. No dead people. No zombies. No demon priest. Just bibles and hymnals and dust.

"Hello, Trey," a voice says softly. It's so quiet at first, I think I imagine it, but the voice repeats itself. "Hello, Trey."

The sound shakes me. I spin around toward the altar again and the streak of light caused by the candle and my movement burns my eyes temporarily. When my vision clears, I don't see anyone.

Then some shuffling off to the side catches my eye. There's an alcove to the right of the altar, and I see a hand wrapped around the edge of the entryway. The candlelight flickers over the stone and the fingers curled around the corner.

"Who's there?" I call out. I'm nervous and ready to run if I need to. But this person clearly knows me, which means I must know them.

"Please don't be alarmed," the voice says. It's a little louder now, but calm and welcoming. When you're not expecting it, though, calm and welcoming can seem downright creepy.

I slide my machete out in preparation for a fight. I hope I don't have to use it again, but what's one more swipe if I need to? I've chopped down more people than I could count today, and one more would make zero difference to me.

I return to the altar, cautious in my movements, and also keeping my wits about me, knowing there could be others lurking in the shadows too. I move up the three steps at the center and move toward the alcove on the side.

"Been looking for you for quite some time," the voice says. And as I get closer, a face leans out from the shadows, into the candlelight.

And it's *my* face.

"Hello, brother."

16

"IT'S BEEN A long time, hasn't it?" the man—my doppelganger—says, still half tucked away behind the edge of the stone wall.

One of my brothers? My knees wobble, and my mind reels, trying to reconcile what I'm seeing. My brothers have been gone—dead—since we were kids. Very young kids.

How is this possible? One of them survived? Was I lied to all those years ago? Have I been grieving and suffering my entire life over something only half true?

He steps out a little more, and stands there, nude, presenting himself to me beside the edge of the wall, as if to give me a moment, a chance to believe that what I'm seeing is real. His face is just like mine. His body is just like mine. It's like looking in a mirror. Even the birthmark on my thigh is on his thigh.

Is this real? Can it be?

"It is," he says. "And there's more for you to see." There's a slight curl to his lip. A smile. Not a crazed smile, but a friendly one. A loving, brotherly smile.

I swallow hard. My throat feels like sandpaper. Suddenly some bile works its way up, and it burns, and I have to swallow again to get rid of it. It's acid on the moment, but I won't let it ruin our reunion.

My brother steps completely out from the alcove, now fully illuminated by the flickering light of the candle on the altar. And my other brother is there too. He walks with a strange sideways movement, like a shuffle, but smoother. It looks odd, but also seems familiar.

I'm stunned. They're *both* alive? Somehow it makes sense. I put my machete away.

Memories flood back from our shared early childhood. My brothers and I eating meals together, our parents dressing us, changing our diapers, teaching us colors. Reading us stories.

Things I probably shouldn't remember because we were so young. But I do.

How many boys? One, two, three! Three little boys! That's right! How many arms? One, two, three, four, five... What comes after five? Six! That's right, boys! So smart!

Then my brothers getting sick, feeling weak, while I felt strong. Them withering. Me thriving.

They step closer to me, moving in tandem, as always. I'm oddly happy to see that they're still attached at the bases of their skulls, and at the tops of their backs and shoulders.

I was right there with them once. I still have the scars. But life is unpredictable, even if it sometimes does come full circle.

I have this memory from early on. Of doctors speaking with my parents in serious, grim tones. Silent tears flowing. Difficult decisions being made. Fear and disappointment and sadness. Grief. Guilt.

I was the only one of the three who had any real chance of survival. I was the one who was growing the way he was supposed to. But it was only because my body was depleting my brothers of what they needed. In a way, I was cannibalizing them, though I was unable to control it.

During one conversation, my parents were told that if the three of us remained attached, it was likely we would all die in a matter of months. Maybe even weeks.

So, in order for me to survive, my brothers had to die. And I've been holding onto the guilt associated with that choice—even though it wasn't my choice—my entire life.

And yet, they survived? Has my entire life been a lie? A joke?

How was this kept from me for so many years? Who knew what I didn't? Why didn't someone find me and tell me and why is this happening now?

My scars tingle. I reach up under the hair on the back of my head and rub one of them with the tips of my fingers.

"You understand what's happening, don't you?" my brothers say. They speak from both mouths, in unison, using one voice. My voice.

And I know the words before they're spoken. I hear them

inside my head before I hear them with my ears.

"Choices are made based on circumstances," we say. "But our choices pollute with their short-sightedness. Pollute everything. Our surroundings, our relationships, our families. So now, something has come in to clean up the mess. To course-correct. To fix it as best they can."

What do they mean, something? Like, some *thing?* Some force? An energy? Or a being?

Oh. It hits me like a ton of bricks. Like a collapsing bell tower.

"How foolish it is to think we're all alone in the universe. How many foolish things we think, every day, just to get ourselves to tomorrow, without ever really preparing for the future."

A smile creeps across my face, slowly. Like a realization.

We—humanity—can't be trusted anymore. The slate is being wiped clean. We're being driven insane, our minds scrambled, our bodies twisted. The mutations make us stronger, but it's only temporary, to aid the buzzing in our brains so we can overpower the others in the short-term.

We're in the way. We're a cancer that needs to be eradicated. The difficult decision has been made, and it's beyond all our control.

It makes me chuckle. It's all so simple, really. A chaos plan. They make us crazy. They make us kill. It won't take long, really. We'll take ourselves out, and probably do it in twenty-four hours or so.

"Is it starting to make a bit more sense?" my brothers and I say to each other.

Did they intend to raise the dead too? That seems like an unintentional side effect. Unless it's meant as a distraction. More chaos.

I scratch the scar at the base of my skull, tracing it down the back of my neck. There are other scars, on my shoulders, down either side of my spine. Where my brothers and I all used to be attached. They itch too, but not as much.

My brothers step toward me, their movements perfectly cooperative, as if they are of one mind. Which I suppose we are.

"It would seem a few of us are immune to the plan, however. Immune to the gas, and to the madness that is unfolding around us. Perhaps that's how we three have made it this long."

Could that be? Is someone, or something, going to come take us away? Is there somewhere else we can go? Somewhere habitable we can live, maybe even thrive, even if it's with creatures completely unlike us, from somewhere else in the universe? The possibilities are mind-boggling. I scratch my chin like I'm thinking, but it's really just the itch.

Why are we—my brothers and I—the lucky ones? Why do we get to survive? What's so special about us? What an absurd thought. It makes me laugh.

My scars are agitated. On fire. They feel intensely warm to the touch now, radiating heat I can feel with my fingers and down past my wrists. They're itchy. Swollen. I hack at the one behind my head with my hands, clawing away at it, breaking the skin and nearly pulling the nails off my fingertips.

My brothers side-step around me, then place their backs against my own and it feels exactly like it did when we were kids.

There's a deep rumbling sound up above, and all around us, breaking through the quiet of the church's sanctuary. Suddenly the stone walls begin to vibrate. Dust shakes free. I inhale the musty smell and the scent of my brothers and feel the rumble deep inside my bones. Our bones. It feels like an earthquake. Like a body quake. It's coming from within and without.

"I think it will be nice," my brothers and I say, in a fit of hilarity that begins to take hold, all of us now approaching ecstatic laughter, our bodies quivering—our one-two-three-four-five-*six* hands scratching away at our one-two-*three* necks—the burning, itching, sizzling fire exploding in our one, one—*ONE!*—mind.

Our backs bubble out, and burst, and fuse.

Just like old times.

We're so happy to be with each other again, thrilled to be starting our new/old life together. I promise to be a better partner. I promise to nurture and not drain you/us. We will be the best we've ever been and grow better together than we ever could apart.

I look up and feel my eyes rolling—*our* eyes rolling—spinning, as a circle of blue-white light forms directly above us, first outside from above and through the hazy sky, then shooting down through the vaulted ceiling of the church, a column of light penetrating the stone, and illuminating us like a brilliant spotlight. My knees—*our* knees—are no longer wobbling, nor are they supporting us. Suddenly we're rising up into the air, weightless. Our scars itch fiercely, but it's the only physical sensation we feel anymore.

Then we remember the blade on our back and wonder if that will help soothe the itch. We pull the machete from the sheath and raise it high with all six of our hands around the handle, then drag it down across our necks.

And as we pass through the ceiling of the stone church, like a ghost—*one* ghost—and float into the darkened haze above, we can't see where we're headed, except into a great void, and we don't even care.

It's all a big joke, and whether we want to or not, we can't stop laughing.

Acknowledgments

Immense gratitude to my wife, Gina Renzi, and my author-brothers, Adam Cesare, Matt Serafini, Patrick Lacey, and Aaron Dries. Huge thanks also to C.V. Hunt and Andersen Prunty for taking this story on, and helping to tweak and twist it into its final form, and to Shawn Macomber for the fantastic blurb which adorns the cover.

Scott Cole is a writer, artist, and graphic designer living in Philadelphia.

He likes old radio dramas, old horror comics, weird movies, cold weather, coffee, and a few other things too.

Find him on social media, or at 13visions.com

Other Grindhouse Press Titles
#666__*Satanic Summer* by Andersen Prunty
#064__*Blood Relations* by Kristopher Triana
#063__*The Perfectly Fine House* by Stephen Kozeniewski and Wile E. Young
#062__*Savage Mountain* by John Quick
#061__*Cocksucker* by Lucas Milliron
#060__*Luciferin* by J. Peter W.
#059__*The Fucking Zombie Apocalypse* by Bryan Smith
#058__*True Crime* by Samantha Kolesnik
#057__*The Cycle* by John Wayne Comunale
#056__*A Voice So Soft* by Patrick Lacey
#055__*Merciless* by Bryan Smith
#054__*The Long Shadows of October* by Kristopher Triana
#053__*House of Blood* by Bryan Smith
#052__*The Freakshow* by Bryan Smith
#051__*Dirty Rotten Hippies and Other Stories* by Bryan Smith
#050__*Rites of Extinction* by Matt Serafini
#049__*Saint Sadist* by Lucas Mangum
#048__*Neon Dies at Dawn* by Andersen Prunty
#047__*Halloween Fiend* by C.V. Hunt
#046__*Limbs: A Love Story* by Tim Meyer
#045__*As Seen On T.V.* by John Wayne Comunale
#044__*Where Stars Won't Shine* by Patrick Lacey
#043__*Kinfolk* by Matt Kurtz
#042__*Kill For Satan!* by Bryan Smith
#041__*Dead Stripper Storage* by Bryan Smith
#040__*Triple Axe* by Scott Cole
#039__*Scummer* by John Wayne Comunale
#038__*Cockblock* by C.V. Hunt
#037__*Irrationalia* by Andersen Prunty
#036__*Full Brutal* by Kristopher Triana
#035__*Office Mutant* by Pete Risley
#034__*Death Pacts and Left-Hand Paths* by John Wayne Comunale
#033__*Home Is Where the Horror Is* by C.V. Hunt
#032__*This Town Needs A Monster* by Andersen Prunty

#031___*The Fetishists* by A.S. Coomer
#030___*Ritualistic Human Sacrifice* by C.V. Hunt
#029___*The Atrocity Vendor* by Nick Cato
#028___*Burn Down the House and Everyone In It* by Zachary T. Owen
#027___*Misery and Death and Everything Depressing* by C.V. Hunt
#026___*Naked Friends* by Justin Grimbol
#025___*Ghost Chant* by Gina Ranalli
#024___*Hearers of the Constant Hum* by William Pauley III
#023___*Hell's Waiting Room* by C.V. Hunt
#022___*Creep House: Horror Stories* by Andersen Prunty
#021___*Other People's Shit* by C.V. Hunt
#020___*The Party Lords* by Justin Grimbol
#019___*Sociopaths In Love* by Andersen Prunty
#018___*The Last Porno Theater* by Nick Cato
#017___*Zombieville* by C.V. Hunt
#016___*Samurai Vs. Robo-Dick* by Steve Lowe
#015___*The Warm Glow of Happy Homes* by Andersen Prunty
#014___*How To Kill Yourself* by C.V. Hunt
#013___*Bury the Children in the Yard: Horror Stories* by Andersen Prunty
#012___*Return to Devil Town (Vampires in Devil Town Book Three)* by Wayne Hixon
#011___*Pray You Die Alone: Horror Stories* by Andersen Prunty
#010___*King of the Perverts* by Steve Lowe
#009___*Sunruined: Horror Stories* by Andersen Prunty
#008___*Bright Black Moon (Vampires in Devil Town Book Two)* by Wayne Hixon
#007___*Hi I'm a Social Disease: Horror Stories* by Andersen Prunty
#006___*A Life On Fire* by Chris Bowsman
#005___*The Sorrow King* by Andersen Prunty
#004___*The Brothers Crunk* by William Pauley III
#003___*The Horribles* by Nathaniel Lambert
#002___*Vampires in Devil Town* by Wayne Hixon
#001___*House of Fallen Trees* by Gina Ranalli
#000___*Morning is Dead* by Andersen Prunty

Printed in Great Britain
by Amazon